Table of Contents

You can hear many of the authors in this issue read their stories, poems, and essays at https://soundcloud.com/tahomaliterary/tracks.

About This Issue

How do we live now? I feel our contributors asking—even shouting—this question throughout these pages. How do we live amid the specters of the pandemic, of cataclysmic climate events, of systemic racism? This issue's contributors discuss the power and poetry of living in a body; they discuss grief, aging, first sexual experiences, the struggles of immigrant life. Then there's coming to terms with life, period, seeking connection in the cosmic void.

I'm no longer surprised when I sit down to pursue an essay and my mother, who has been dead for twenty years, pops into my writing. The topic could be anything—canoeing, the mystery of a discarded shoe, the male gaze—and up she shows. Here she is, reminding me not to squint. *Are you sure you have enough light?* I can't escape her, and our connection was such that I don't want to. It seems that I'm not alone, as mothers—and parenting in myriad forms—take a central role in many of the twenty-eight poems, stories, and essays collected here. Contributors explore a woman's right to choose to be or not to be a mother. They explore child bearing, child rearing, growing to become our parents, caring for aging parents, and losing those we love. These themes of families and relationships are variations of that overarching question: How do we live? How do we live in families?

We hope you'll connect with many of these selections individually, but also with the issue as a whole. We hope that it will inspire you, as it has us. When the opportunity arises, we'd love to discuss it with you. How *do* we live now?

–Ann Beman, TLR co-publisher and nonfiction editor

We are sad to bid farewell to longtime Poetry Editor Mare Heron Hake, as her other obligations have changed. While this is her last issue with us, the break-up is both amicable and unavoidable. She's promised to still be a part of social media, and to send her a message you can contact us through our website. We'll be sure she sees it.

In the happier part of this change, we're very excited that Jessica Cuello is staying with us as full Editor of the genre, with two associate editors joining her for Issue 25.

We hope you enjoy the original fiction, nonfiction, and poetry in this issue. As ever, let us know what you think. We're on Twitter, Facebook, and Instagram.

Part of our commitment as editors and publishers is to present a broad range of voices and topics. At times, our selections may be graphic; characters may be profane and scenes may be explicit. Some selections may make us uncomfortable, but we believe that a purpose of literature is to push boundaries of what we know, understand, or assume.

We will not publish material that endorses harm to others or that encourages prejudice. Whenever the magazine's selections depict violence, include explicit words or describe sexual acts we include them because we believe they serve a purpose other than to merely titillate or to offend.

TAHOMA
LITERARY
REVIEW

A Posse of Parables:
A series of 100-word stories
JULIA HALPRIN JACKSON

Home school

You give me homework, he said. And I give you homework. And that's how we do school. She dreamed big and assigned him the moon. Too far, silly, he said. Fine, then: she assigned him the coral reef. Too deep. All right, she said. Catch a Bengal tiger. Too dangerous. Here, let me show you. He gave her a notebook and a pencil and a seat under a willow tree. Write what you want to learn, he said. She mapped the night sky with imaginary constellations. Write something real, he growled. Something real, she wrote. He disappeared. She continued writing.

Workshop

It's a relationship of subordination, one poet says to another. She—the speaker—expresses guilt, see, and he—the listener—demands something. Money, maybe, sex. No, says another student, what we have here is a special form of tenderness. Someone hums Bowie. A door creaks shut. What throws me, says the teacher, is the penguin—what's *he* doing here? What do you mean, *he*? asks another. The poet, the guilty one, stays quiet, her iceberg hidden. They are blind to her but still they spear her to the page. She considers prostration in all its poetic forms, though her wings stay close to her chest.

Career Day

Janie stopped by the Career Fair to pick up a career. It was easier than she thought. First she took an aptitude test, which narrowed her down to flower-arranging or graveyard digging. Then she got to meet professional flower arrangers and gravediggers. There were pirates, too, and badminton delegates from Canada. Someone offered to compost her resume. A photographer took her headshot as she swatted away birdies. Don't worry, Janie, they all said, work hard and the right opportunity will come to you. You could even arrange flowers above graves! She left with a packet of seeds and a shovel.

Cover letter

To Whom it May Concern:

Please consider me for _____ position at _____ company. I believe I am qualified to _____ because of my considerable experience as a _____, _____ and _____. My interest in _____, as well as my dedication and commitment to _____, are in line with _____'s mission to be a _____ and _____ company of the future. If hired, I promise to _____, _____ and _____. I'll ____ what you want me to ____, ____ when you say ____. I will make you money. Don't worry about how.

Thank you for your consideration.

Sincerely,

_____ _____

Postcard

Dear You,

It's yourself, further away than you thought. You're somewhere where your difference is heightened, where your height is different, your carriage diminished by buildings older and stories more dignified than you. You smell orange blossoms and milky coffee and your arms itch with travel. You miss home, but soon your home will travel to meet you. You'll merge with air currents above the Atlantic where both of you—*us*—combine, refract, and slide over each other, a photograph's negative, as our histories trade, and you are here, and you are there, reading this.

Wish you were here.
You Know Who

Fortune cookie

You never used to like figs and now there's purple juice dripping down your chin. You drink red wine from your father's glass. You listen to public radio and know the farmers at the market. You sense innate parental mimicry: clenching your jaw in traffic, running your fingers along the tablecloth, murmuring as you read the news. No amount of separation can deny a jawline, the length of your fingers or the lines on your forehead. You thought inheritance was a debt you had to repay, but when your daughter hums a nonsense song—your nonsense song—you reach for a fig.

Someone always came in

WILLIAM ARCHILA

Someone always came in with the story they had seen her
a black shape in a tunic, wavering in the mist where light
diminishes, some said horse-faced, some said beauty.
When I was a child, the hag of the crooked river stalked
the woods, the fiery flood of fish on her breath, gritty as silt
some said crow-black hair, some said lost in brambles
but always her tongue curled around the beak breaking feather
& hollow bone, till the cracks of her mouth were nothing
but a mother of wings.
                    So this is what it means to have a survivor
a story that begins wobbling through thicket, hacking at weeds
till it gets ugly. No one has returned to El Mozote, except those
of us who look like fools in the face of the elegy. Except her, back
in a body of coal to exhume the ragged folklore of a ten-year-old.
Here's where I must touch & see. A handkerchief is not enough.

Vixen

Elena M. Aponte

Six years ago, Evie gave birth to two sable-colored fox kits. Wet and shiny, hot on her skin and slicked with blood, they scratched her when the doctor settled them between her breasts. They mewled, loud and urgent, snuffling fluid from their nostrils. This is what she saw, and they are what she held close, and this is what she told Shane for many days, straining for her kits in their little plastic cribs next to her hospital bed. She wanted them close. She wanted to nurse them and fall asleep with them kneading and tugging. They couldn't regulate their own body temperature and she shouted this at him when he told her about her incision and held down her shoulders to tell her she couldn't do that, and what was she talking about and please, Evie, please what's wrong with you.

The nurses found her drenched in sweat, scrabbling at the plastic cribs, desperate to feed her screaming babies as blood trickled down her leg. Shane shouted in the hallway for someone to help, that she'd "gone crazy or something." Postpartum endometriosis almost killed her. She was delirious from infection, from the lingering pain of childbirth, the grief of the babies she'd lost before.

But even after she and the boys settled into a rhythm, she'd lie awake at night feeding them both together on each breast and feel a primal current run through her, something she couldn't explain and would never feel again. And each time, she remembered the kits. How she'd birthed two glossy and beautiful little creatures, their thick dark fur destined to turn red gold. And then she wept.

"Momma, I want the cinnamon sticks this time," Connor reminds her. He's already sprinkled with a fine dusting of sand and loam and bits of blackish dirt. Reese bounds around him, ripping up grass and holding it above his brother's head, watching the blades spiral down to his face. Connor spits dirt from his mouth and Reese laughs. Evie gives him a warning look and Reese sits on his hands. She grabs a cluster of the fallen branches she's collected for Green Yard Waste pickup and breaks them in half. "It's sassafras," she says. "It just smells like cinnamon. They used to make root beer out of it."

She arranges the broken sticks carefully across Connor's torso and he wrinkles his nose.

"That sounds gross."

Reese pokes at a few rocks with a sassafras branch she gives him. "Like how some tea is made from flowers?"

"Exactly."

Connor sneezes and wipes his nose with the back of his arm. "I want to make ice cream from it instead. Like with the mochi."

Evie smiles as she gathers more sticks to toss into the battered waste bin. Connor is the one who was really enamored with his summer camp exercises; his favorite involves lying on the grass and being covered gently with things from nature, so that he feels more and more comfortable with it. He also came back from camp with a ravenous appetite for mochi ice cream. His favorite flavor is matcha, of all things. Reese prefers chocolate, ever her little realist. Both have heads of full dark hair, though Reese's is a shade lighter, with more auburn. They each inherited her pointed nose, which they'll only grow into by the time they're sixteen. Sometimes when the summer sun shines behind their pointed ears and lights them red, she thinks of the foxes.

"Hey you know what," Reese says. "We haven't seen Ella in a while."

Evie's smile falters. "She's really busy with some eaglets right now. We don't want to—"

"Eaglets!" Connor sits up and a puff of dust bursts into the air behind him. She hopes sincerely he hasn't somehow covered himself in spores. "I wanna see 'em!"

"Yeah, me too. We haven't been in forever, Momma."

It pains her to deny them something they're so excited about. She hasn't been to work in a few days under the pretense of catching a cold. The angry red marks on her forearms have just started to fade, and she bought a new shade of foundation that would match the skin there perfectly. She knew what Ella would say if she saw anything was amiss. Evie wasn't ready to hear it.

"What kind of eaglets are they?" Connor asks her. He grabs her hand and dirt smears across her palm and he smells like the forest and her heart cracks open for him.

"Golden," she says. "They hatched about a week ago."

"Golden eagles!" Reese says. She swears his voice has gone up an octave. "We gotta see them, Mom. You said they won't be back until the spring!"

"Please let's go!"

Evie can't bear to refuse them. She yearns to see the little ones, too, and for her boys to lay eyes on such a fragile and private thing. With the assurance that they wash up before she takes them, the boys run inside and talk excitedly between themselves. Meanwhile, Evie rummages through the Walgreens bags she's hidden underneath the sink for her brand-new tube of liquid foundation, Ivory Number 2.

The first time she and Shane visited the Upper Peninsula, they were young and scared of bears, excited to spend time together in the wilderness and make love under ferns and pines. Evie had fallen in love so thoroughly, and their talk of marriage transformed into a game of what ifs. What if they lived up here? What if they started their own business? What if they rescued animals? And when Shane proposed they were swimming in the cold lake together, freezing and laughing and staring into each other's eyes. Mist on the still water of the bay behind them. The pines swaying. He gave her a Petoskey stone and told her to wait for a ring. When she eventually showed her mother the petite, pretty diamond her mother pulled her close into a wordless hug. It wasn't disappointment or relief, but it wasn't happiness either, and they looked at each other, really, as if for the first time.

"Don't, Evelyn," her mother said.

She had felt cold, unmoored, lost, knowing her mother believed she was doing nothing that made sense. No teaching, no PhD program. About to marry a wildman, using her spare time to coax rare birds into copulating in safety, wrestling with abandoned lynx cubs and getting bit by stoats. She was so far away from home, so far above the fingers of the mitten-shaped Michigan they knew so well, far from the winding cobbled roads of Ann Arbor where she'd grown up.

It was wild in the U.P., forests thick with pine, swamp, and cedar. Evie and Shane's romantic engagement had inspired dreams of living in a cabin with no internet and taking trade jobs that would make them each enough to get by. Shane could start a restoration business, having spent so many years laying bricks, hammering drywall, leveling support beams and tearing up piles and piles of old hardwood flooring. Evie would have her wildlife rehab and science center, filled with foxes, sables, and chinchillas rescued from fur farms, and little sanctuaries for abandoned wild babies.

It was all so sweet, so very much the hopes and dreams of two young kids in love, and they might have been able to actually do it. When she caught word of a wildlife refuge looking for rangers near Marquette, a city nestled against Lake Superior, she jumped at the chance. But Shane wasn't as happy as she'd hoped he'd be.

Shane loved her because of her ambition, it was true. He loved her because she was smart and cunning and witty and could run fast and swim for hours. He loved her because she was a swipe and grab away with his long arms and wide hands, and when his rough fingers closed around her soft skin he relished the feeling of her muscle tensing, her fingers clawing. Shane liked to play games and play rough, and he liked to chase her, find her in her quiet moments and pull her into his arms or the bed or the slate grey surface of the lake on overcast days.

Now he forgets things on purpose, tells her that sending the boys into the woods for so many hours each day, each season, is pointless until they are older. The man who once picked up feed apples during the summer from the roadside stand at the crux of the bike trails and threw them into the tree line to feed the deer. The man who caught spiders and stink bugs in a paper cup and tossed them into the bushes outside is now only mildly interested in the little fossils his sons find by the creek bed, the impressions of seashells or the swirl of a snail caught forever in stone.

Evie is afraid that she hates him for this. The boys grew up with so many things she did not. They help her plant cucumbers and carrots and tomatoes and eggplants in the spring. They love to put their hands in mud and water the wild knot of poppies alongside the house and look for frogs. She shares their excitement as they discover things for the first time. But they change around Shane, now. They yearn to impress him, and they start to play rough, too, and gnash their teeth and yank hair and tear holes in their jeans.

Shane was never like this before them. Before them he was sweet and soft inside. The problem is and always was, he'd tell her sometimes in the insolated darkness of their bedroom, that he wasn't ready for two at a time. He never was. Can never be sure if he ever will be. Evie, who had felt them move at fifteen weeks, whose petite frame bloated to accommodate them, had always been ready.

Ella is all smiles when she sees Connor and Reese tumble through the sanctuary gates, racing each other to get up to her. They look a little ridiculous in their new fall coats, oversized as they are on their skinny frames. They are growing so fast, too fast. Evie knows she'll cry the first time one of them gets as tall as her shoulder. She doesn't want them to grow, not yet. Right now they are her little ones, her little kits, and she can never resist the urge to keep them clean, warm, and bundled close.

When she walks up to Ella, her hands in her pockets, the wind chills her face. Her heart races just a little, knowing that the marks are covered with a layer of foundation and her coat sleeves, but worried that somehow Ella can see it with X-ray eyes.

"Ella! Ella!" Connor says. "We're here to see the babies!"

She picks him up in a hug and Reese waits excitedly next to her for his turn. Evie edges closer to them, feeling like she's edging into a life that used to be hers—a smiling woman juggling children, animal musk clinging to her sweaty skin. Leaves skitter across the ground between Ella's mud-caked boots.

"I hope we're ready to wash our hands," she tells the boys. "These babies are freshly baked. Momma might not even let you touch 'em."

"No, we gotta see 'em. Gold eagles won't come back 'til spring," Reese says.

Evie can't help but laugh. Anything she tells Reese, no matter what it is, even if he overhears her saying something to herself, he'll repeat it to someone else eventually. Ella swings Connor to the ground and grabs up his hand, then Reese's.

"All right. Let's go."

She looks back at Evie as they walk toward the nesting house. "How are you feeling?"

"Better." She says it too fast. Almost before Ella can even finish. A hot flash runs through her. She must keep her head. For god's sake. She's done this kind of hiding before. Her thoughts collide into each other, reading too much into Ella's eyebrow raising, the hurried skipping steps of her sons running ahead of them to the eaglets.

"You sure?" Ella counters.

"Yeah. I'm just tired."

The tried and true response. Evie is almost sorry she's used it. She feels the uncertainty rolling off her friend in waves, this woman who was with her from the beginning, who didn't call her crazy when she said things would be rough when they started, but they could make it work. The woman who once helped her capture a wounded porcupine. The woman who took her to the hospital when she went into labor, driving through the backwoods in a Jeep that clipped a tree stump on the way and still kept going. The only one who didn't blink when she told her about what she gave birth to, and what she'd held in her arms. Evie bows her head and follows her children inside the warm building. At the smell of hay and cedar chips, the smell of life fostering and blooming, her heart feels a little bit lighter.

The vixen appeared once in her dreams, lying in dappled sunlight under the pines where they first met, her broken leg twisted and belly swollen with an impending litter. She was pregnant with three and one would be born still. The other two would be born at the refuge, in Evie's hands, to the smiling delight of her colleagues, who have all waited for this moment—this assurance that what they're doing is right and worth it and they haven't fielded calls from worried housewives about the bird that crashed into their front window for nothing. And the kits were beautiful. Hot, wet, impossibly small, and the vixen took them and licked them furiously, ate their placentas, and lay there, spent, while they suckled. Evie was ten weeks pregnant when she helped deliver the kits.

Foxes are monogamous, and most mate for life. Back then, she admired this about them. It was romantic. To see how the vixen and her tod nuzzled each other while lazing in the fields at the edge of the refuge, the delicate ways in which they groomed and played with each other while she was pregnant—it was almost too much. They were animals doing what they knew how to do, and it shouldn't have mattered, except to Evie it was an embarrassing reflection of her own desperate need. Love wasn't something she took lightly. To see it in such a raw way between the two foxes gnawing at fleas on each other's paws, it was so simple it brought tears to her eyes. She longed to sleep in a heap with Shane, wound in sheets and skin and hot breath and hair, because they belonged to each other. But he started to pull away while she was pregnant, after he felt the first kicks of life against his palm. He did not like when the kids slept in the bed, annoyed by their warm little bodies and their sleep talking and their fluttering eyelids.

She wants to know so badly what hurt him, but he refuses to tell her.

Shane is unhappy, moody, when they return. Evie sends the boys outside to play again since they won't go to their rooms, buzzing with excitement. They still smell faintly like cedar chips and down. Their ears are cold as she presses a kiss to each of them before they run back outside, coats swishing. She feels Shane's eyes on her the whole time. What is he thinking? What's brewing inside him? When she looks at him, he seems like the man she wanted to marry, with his warm brown eyes and long lashes, maybe with more rounded shoulders after he settled into parenthood. Doesn't he like the way she's filled out, how her body has fed his children? He once said breast feeding was gross. She squirted milk in his eye to shut him up and he was furious at her for hours, but it had been funny then. They didn't know what they were doing. She forgave him for his ignorance when she, too, was trying her best with nothing to work from.

"Are you still mad at me?" he asks.

Evie frowns. "I'm not."

"Why weren't you all here when I came home?"

"The boys wanted to see Ella. I couldn't tell them no."

She can't look at him because she is afraid. That's the difference. There are strange molecules in the air now, a sour taste in her mouth. The man she loves feels like a stranger in her home. Like he doesn't belong. "Don't lie, Evie," he says. "You didn't want to see me today. Because of what happened."

She grips the edge of the sink and looks through the window. Connor is at the top of the slide in the back yard and Reese has dumped all of the yard waste from the bin on the ground, searching for the largest stick he can find. "That isn't true."

"I need to see my kids," Shane says.

"I know that," she tells him, and doesn't bother to hide the hint of venom in her voice. The sink is piled with pots and pans from their spaghetti dinner two nights ago. Evie turns on the faucet, dumps dish soap inside and watches it foam. Outside, Reese has found a suitable stick and swings it at his brother, who is still at the top of the slide. Evie dunks her hands into the greasy pans and starts scrubbing with a sponge.

"Then why were you gone?"

"I wasn't trying to avoid you," Evie says. "I texted you."

"When you knew I wouldn't have service at the site?"

They rarely fight like this. Most of the time they are direct and obvious and follow a familiar rhythm. This is clipped and weird, unexpected. He's looking for causalities that aren't there, projecting his guilt, ashamed. Evie sets her jaw as she scrubs sauce from the corner of her pasta pot. The fermented tomato smell is too strong, and she coughs.

"I wasn't trying to avoid you," she repeats.

The silence is charged between them. If they were foxes, they'd be dancing around each other, ears flat against their skulls, teeth bared. Waiting for the first strike or the first opening to run. Evie keeps scrubbing. The faucet is spewing water so hot it steams her face. The boys laugh at each other and their voices echo into the woods. Shane shifts his weight from foot to foot.

"I've apologized so many times," he says.

The leftover tomato sauce sluices into the drain. Evie shuts off the faucet and reaches for a towel. Shane watches her, waiting for her to say something. When she doesn't, he curses to himself. "It was an accident."

She dries the pot and sets it back on the stove. He's growing impatient. She waits. Wanting to know what he'll do next.

"I grabbed your arm," he said. "It's not liked I slapped you."

She rounds on him. "You. Left. A. Mark on me. It hurt. If you had done that to me ten years ago, I would have left you. No questions. No nothing."

Static fills her thoughts. Her ears ring. She's said the thing she was afraid of saying and now she's terrified. His expression has changed. Evie can't bear to face him. She runs from the kitchen to the back door into the yard where Connor and Reese are still playing, still laughing. Shane follows and she wishes he wouldn't. She wishes he'd stay in that kitchen and never come out, that she could rip this moment from her life and bury it deep, like she'd buried her babies before.

Three weeks after the vixen and her kits were cleared for re-release, she found the babies about a mile from the refuge, a few feet from the road where the grass thinned into thistle. They looked like they were sleeping, but she knew better. She stopped her car and headed toward them, one hand on her belly, tears welling in her eyes. They had strayed too far from the den, just enough. Their fur had only started to turn, and their white tipped tales looked like ratty paintbrushes. They were still soft to the touch. She cried so hard, until she felt heavy in her chest, as if something had broken and the only thing keeping her heart beating was the anxious swirl of the twins inside her. It was first time she had ever felt them move. The rush of life inside was fluttering and bizarre, beautiful. She buried the little ones where they had fallen, digging until her nails bled, her skin wrinkled with dirt, and marked their graves with small cairns. She didn't see the vixen or her mate ever again.

"Evie!"

Fear blurs her peripherals, but she can sense the kids to her left, over on the swing set. She runs for the tree line, past their raised gardens full of eggplants.

"Evie, stop!"

Shane seizes her wrist. She spins fast to twist from him. He pulls her hard, and she almost falls. Reese calls out to her. Connor calls for Shane, confused.

"Evie. The boys are watching."

"Don't," she demands, wrenching her arm away.

"Momma—"

"Get inside," Shane shouts at them. "Now."

Evie's heart races. She feels dizzy. The boys scrabble around the raised beds, trying to get closer. All she wants to do is run into the trees. Her chest burns. Sobs threaten to wrench from inside her. Reese appears in front of her, hands upturned, like he wants her to lift him into her arms. She grabs him up instinctively. Connor lunges for them, his voice reedy and worried, afraid she'll leave him behind. She grabs his hand. For a brief moment she sees the clarity of her choice, with both of her children pressed into her, and she feels relief at the thought they might go forward into the leaves with her, and cobwebs might collect in their hair, and she might come out the other side stronger and different and better. She is close enough for a pine tree to scratch at her bare arms before Shane tears Reese from her hold. She stumbles. He yanks Connor away. Evie trips. The boys cry out as she falls hard to the dirt.

"What is wrong with you?" Shane says.

She coughs. Tears sting at the corners of her eyes. The boys struggle in Shane's grasp, confused and ready to cry themselves. Her stomach roils. A fire has replaced her fear, threatening to spill over. He's roughed up their children. Her children.

She sees the flash of something in the trees—fast, brilliant, like a beacon. An eye. Green, then yellow. A predator. Quick moving. Reese pulls out of his jacket and runs to her, straining his arms for an embrace. She collects him, presses him to her chest, curls around him. Connor sobs, wanting her but unable to break free from Shane's grip on his arm. Through the screen of Reese's hair, Evie watches the floating eyes settle into a skull, a familiar angular face, all triangles, built for reception, perception, decision. It's dark enough that the pale glow from the kitchen lights illuminates a slice of the yard, enough to see the brilliant auburn coat of the vixen as she bounds forward past the upturned waste can, past the swing set, toward Shane and Connor.

"Momma," Reese whispers.

Shane finally sees her, now, slow as always, and is so shocked to see a fox running toward him that he releases Connor and scrambles away. Evie sits up, still clutching Reese, and watches the vixen stop a few feet away from her other son. Shane shouts at the fox and she starts but doesn't run. Her ears flatten on her head. Connor gathers himself from the ground and runs toward Evie. He falls into her arms, hugging her fiercely. Her heart roars in her ears. Tears are hot and bright on her face.

"You haven't changed," she says. The vixen's left ear twitches, as if she's heard her voice. Shane shouts again but the little fox holds her ground. Her tail swishes across the leaves. Shane stoops, seizes a fistful of mulch, and throws it at her. Still, she doesn't move. She's mere feet from where Evie and the children lie in a heap, watching. Her amber eyes shine green as she looks back at them. Evie is so relieved to see her, so full of joy, but the children are angry at their father.

"Don't hurt her!" Connor shouts.

"Leave her alone!" Reese demands.

"I can't fucking move," Shane counters.

The children flinch. Evie squeezes their arms reassuringly.

"She won't hurt you," Evie tells him. Her voice is clear and even, now. Shane doesn't seem to understand. Foxes do not attack people. They are wired for curiosity and suspicion and mischief. They want nothing more than a meal and affection. She's seen them eat twinkies and discarded French fries. She's seen them play with old dolls and bits of aluminum foil. They're nothing if not childish. But Shane is angry, humiliated, upset that his children defended their mother. He bends down for a rock. The boys plead with him as he cocks his arm back for a throw. Evie hurries to her feet, unsteady in the tangle of their limbs, not sure what she's about to do, what she can do, if she can do it. A horrible, strangling bark echoes through the yard before she can say anything. A fox call. One she recognizes immediately. The male slinks into the dim light, thicker, larger, dense fur, lip curled enough to remind them his kind, intelligent face can shift to protect at any moment.

"Shane," Evie says. "Go inside. Leave us be."

There is a long moment where he stares at them, takes them all in, takes everything in. The deafening cheer of crickets, the flick of the vixen's tail through the grass, the male's low and disapproving rumble, the wild stink of them, the boys sniffling, and Evie staring back at him with tears drying on her face.

"Go," she says.

It takes him almost too long to drop the rock in his hand, for him to consider her request—absurd as it is with the children whimpering and the foxes staring at him—but he shakes his head and stalks back to the house. The kitchen door slams behind him. The male fox edges closer to the vixen, pokes the corner of mouth and she yawns, showing teeth. Blood pounds behind Evie's eyes and she hangs her head. No more tears, just exhausted. Reese and Connor are quiet, breathing, whimpering. Watching. She brings them close to her and presses kisses into their faces.

"Don't be afraid," she tells them.

"We aren't, Momma," Reese says.

"We aren't," Connor says.

Evie isn't sure how long she sits there with her boys, how long the foxes linger in the yard, nudging sticks with their noses, circling close enough to sniff their hair. She isn't sure what comes next, how to move forward, but one hole in her heart has sealed, repaired itself, now that she's reunited with her friends, her kits, and their kin.

OPEN, PERSEPHONE ATE IT

SHERRE VERNON

for this dark season, the soul
is just atoms, birdwings, seeds. the click
of the morning into my teeth. what is as good
as something broken there, standing
in the dirtbrick yard? O my daughter:
lightchild. will you mourn a decade of bursting?
heartbrave, my daughter of spring has begun
to fear death. today it is the blue shirt. tomorrow
the eventual return to start-stuff. when I am
home she digs, she wakes up crying. alone. I leave
the studio. she pulls the fruit from the bush, the seeds
spilling out, out she sings to the door left open. let the whole
song in. with her hands she diffuses me. bending sideways & breathing
shallow into my bones. softfever. restraint. a distortion of doorways for sunlight
on white paint. sun-glint. say more: gladsome in eucalyptus bath. now *Eu*, you, I want
to mean good. gold. & you & I. & we. are all somehow this stumbled *Eve*, nose to the dirt,
calling after the woman brave enough to leave.

KILLING TIME
CAITE MCNEIL

December in Maine. No snow yet, so the Christmas lights in people's yards are the only source of cheer. But it's morning now and most of the Christmas lights are off. The sky is a matte gray, and it matches the salt-sprayed road, matches my breath. My Subaru's engine struggles in the cold and an emphysemic rattle happens when I shift from first to second gear. I've become adept at ignoring the check-engine light that has been on since Halloween, but this morning on our drive to school, my three-year-old proves to be a more conscientious car owner than I.

"That orange light is blinking now, Mama. What's it telling you?" she says from her spot in the back. Her car seat raises her up significantly and has the effect of a throne or a tennis umpire's chair. Sometimes I can't help but feel like she sits in judgment back there. Bowie the dog shifts in his bed on the seat next to her and grumbles in agreement.

"Huh," I say. "You're right. It wasn't blinking before. I guess it's saying, 'I'm thirsty for new oil! Feed me, Nina. Feeeeeeed Meeee!'" I lower my register to sound like Cookie Monster or the man-eating plant from *Little Shop of Horrors*.

It's so gray out, and I'm tired, and here I am back in the car making the same drive as the day before. If it weren't for my child, I would give into that early morning, pre-coffee, cold, scratchy-throated pessimism that's so easy in winter in Maine. She reminds me to be playful and perky, though it's a tall order on a morning such as this.

"That's silly, Mama. Cars can't drink!" She shakes her head while she looks out the window at early winter. "Another Santa!" she yells, pointing to a blowup Santa in someone's front yard. "But uh-oh! All his reindeer are dead!"

It's true. Santa's reindeer lie scattered behind him like Christmas carnage. Someone forgot to turn-on the reindeer this morning, or maybe they forgot to turn-off the Santa last night. Santa jerks and sways in the wind, waving to passersby, oblivious to the horrors on display right behind him.

If you're going to do Christmas decorations, do them right, I think.

Blink...blink goes the check-engine light, and Nina's still shaking her head in the backseat. Bowie yawns, grumbles again, and I resolve to make an appointment for an oil change this afternoon.

It's not the money or the time, really. It's the total inconvenience of the errand that I resent. The nearest garage is too far to walk home from and sits along a stretch of four-lane highway surrounded by other garages, a marine supply store, a dog groomer, a funeral home, and a cemetery. This industrial corridor offers absolutely nothing by way of entertainment. Not that *I* need to be entertained, necessarily. However, Nina will accompany me on this errand; she is the tough customer.

My moderate hopes for the Jiffy Lube lobby are dashed upon entering. Stacks of tires crowd the room and a single folding chair waits in the back corner next to an overturned trash can displaying issues of *Car and Driver* and *US Weekly* from 2012 and 2015 respectively. A handwritten sign taped to the back of the cash register reads: *Sorry No Wi-Fi!*

"Where *are* we, Mama?" asks Nina as she fingers the tire treads and sniffs hard at the overwhelming smell of rubber. It's cutting and chemical, almost sweet. Her mask, one featuring dancing cats, sucks in at the sides when she huffs like this. It is a trick she picked up at school, this mask-huffing. She also picked up hitting, and most annoyingly, a new valley-girl inflected exclamation: "Oh my gaaawwd."

"It's a Jiffy Lube, honey," I chime back, feigning positivity for the guy working the register. Then under my breath: "Don't worry. We're not staying."

Four lanes separate the Jiffy Lube from the cemetery where we'll spend some time, and the cars on this section of highway have no reason to slow. As we cross, the wind is sheer bitterness made crueler by the drivers' scornful glances. I have felt this kind of judgment much more acutely since becoming a mother. Mothering in the time of COVID has been one long exercise in weighing the expectations of others against my needs and those of my family.

Yes, I'm taking my child and dog to play in a cemetery. I level flat, beleaguered eyes at the passing cars. The nearest Chuck E. Cheese is fifty miles away, and anyway, there's pandemic in the air and probably a turd in the ball pit.

"Okay crew, let's book it!" I say, sensing an opening in the traffic pattern. I hold Nina's hand in one of mine and she drags behind, not sensing the danger of our crossing. In my other hand, I hold Bowie's leash and he's pulling hard toward the other side of the highway. Bowie, the rescue dog with a well-honed sense of danger, gets it.

Once inside the cemetery's gate, I let Bowie loose, and he and Nina are off running. "Go wild, little beasts!" I say. The cars on the highway zoom past, mere yards away, but there's a chain link fence hemming us in. We're safe here.

It's a Catholic cemetery, and one of the newer ones in this very old Maine town. Many of the names are French Canadian—Belanger, Gamache, St. Onge—and the dates correspond to the town's textile industry boom in the mid nineteenth century. When hundreds of Quebecoise moved to Brunswick, Maine to work in the cotton mills, they founded a Catholic church, and this cemetery soon followed. As poor mill workers, many never had money enough to buy a home. They did, it seems, have just enough to invest in eternity: a resting place in Saint John's.

Nina walks amongst the hundreds of headstones. Their granite cold and worn, their chiseled lettering fading, the stones offer a stark antagonism to my child's warmth, her roundness. "It's sad that so many people are under the ground," she says. The braid she wore to school is coming out at the sides and her mittens hang from her jacket sleeves. I find her most beautiful in this rumpled state. Untidy and gorgeous.

"Well, yes. There are bodies buried here under the ground. But I like to think that the *people* are elsewhere. At least, maybe alive in others' memories of them?"

"That's complicated," she says. And she's right. I'm never ready for her big questions.

That's complicated is another one of her new sayings. She uses it most frequently when describing her classmates' family structures. *Jackson and Eli have two mommies and a daddy. But their mommies are getting a divorce. It's complicated.*

"Mommy," she says, pointing to a larger-than-life crucifix a few rows away. The cross is made of wood, but the corpus itself is painted fiberglass that has been patched in various spots with bent aluminum and finishing nails. Its paint is fading from sun and acid rain. The stigmata are the pink of bubble gum and Jesus' skin is jaundiced and flecked with bird guano.

"Mommy, who's that lady?"

"Oh, that...that's Jesus."

"Why's she crying?"

"Well, I suppose she looks around and sees a lot to cry about."

"I suppose."

I'm reminded of a bumper sticker my father referenced a lot throughout my youth. Driving past a New Hampshire billboard advertising the coming of Christ, my mom would heave this exaggerated sigh, as much for the tackiness of billboards in general as for the inanity of the message. Dad's mouth would turn up at the side and he'd say over his shoulder for my brother and my enter-tainment: "Jesus is coming...and boy is he PISSED!" Hearing our habitually reticent father use a swear word was thrilling. We laughed to ourselves and resumed our backseat reading or Walkman listening, never stopping to consider Jesus the man, the god, nor the sinful state of the world that might have angered him so.

Today, Nina and I are mainly concerned with the puddles collecting in the graveyard's gravel paths, but every now and then Nina notices a cherub, or an angel carved into someone's headstone.

"I like this one," she says as she approaches a grave and traces with her tiny fingers the chiseled shape of the angel of death. The face of the angel is that of a child and is framed by arched wings. *Bloomed on earth to blossom in heaven,* reads the etching. *1855-1858.* The granite is pocked and worn, embellished with chartreuse-colored lichen, but the carving is deep. Still traceable by little fingers. Still legible to this mother who tends to make too much of things.

I won't tell Nina that the grave belongs to a person her age, who probably succumbed to yellow fever, the pandemic of the time, but I will wonder at the way she is drawn to this, out of hundreds of stones. How she tarries, tracing the angel's face and wings, communing with another three-year-old child, only this one's been dead for over a hundred and fifty years. Maybe it's the grayness of this winter day, but I can't shake the image of a blossom—in my mind, something vibrant and ephemeral, a day lily, perhaps.

"Mommy," she says, snapping us out of our reverie. "Knock knock,"

"Who's there?"

"Interrupting cow"

"Interrupting cow wh—"

"Moooooo!"

It's been a hard year. There's a global pandemic still raging, and my daughter is among the unlucky who are still too young for a vaccine. My husband and I work from home, so Nina *needs* to go to preschool. And besides, we rationalize, it's good for her to be social. The trappings of life in the time of COVID no longer faze us. Nose swabs, N95s, daily temperature-taking and intake forms, school closures for close contacts, hand washing till our fingers are cracked and bloody—we take all this in stride. I have friends who judge me for my recklessness, sending an unvaxxed kid into the germ-swirling public. If this plague behaved more like Yellow Fever, I would swaddle myself and my family up in the same white sheet and never leave the house. If this plague took more children, we would all behave much differently. What I don't tell these friends (though they probably already know) is that I'm not patient enough to spend all day with my toddler. She's already learned all her swear words from me and she uses them with aplomb, a fact which fills me with both pride and embarrassment. "Mommy, my damn socks don't match!" she said last week. At last Thanksgiving: "Ronald Reagan? What an asshole."

My husband and I joke that if Nina and I spent every day together, she would enter kindergarten with a strong vocabulary, yes, but an *adult* vocabulary that we would hear about come conference time. But I worry that if Nina and I spent every day together, I would get nothing done. I would sour to motherhood and grow to resent her constant questions, her constant needs. The only reason I *am* a good mother is because I get a daily break from her.

I'm not *unafraid* of the virus. It keeps me up a lot of nights. And since COVID hit, my health, something I have always taken for granted, has been shit. Check engine: five MRIs, four ultrasounds and three CT scans later, and I still don't know why my hands, feet, jaw and left thigh sometimes go numb. Why there's a constant stabbing feeling coming from under my right ribs. I take so many pills I must store them in one of those days of the week pill sorters my grandmother used at the end. My doctors are stumped, and my Google search history would take one on a tour of the most common to the most obscure illnesses in the land. I don't recommend this tour to anyone. In the end, it only makes you think of death.

So I think about death all the time. I dread it for its darkness, its loneliness, its lack. I am afraid to die and leave Nina motherless. I imagine the sadness she would carry around with her, slumped shoulders, a weak diaphragm. I imagine the projections of pity others would lay upon her. *She's shy because she lost her mother, poor dear. She never learned her four times tables because that's the month her mother died, poor girl.* My husband would be wonderful, burdened by sadness, but he would rise to the challenges of training bras, tampons, and relational aggression among teenage girls. He would be everything she needed. Jealousy toward the living enters my morbid musings frequently.

Worse than contemplating my own death, I am afraid that Nina will die and leave me childless. Even my husband couldn't save me from the despair I would feel if I lost Nina. I don't think I could tolerate any kind of bodily contact, no matter how tender. Every touch would remind me of motherhood, of the person I would cease to be. These breasts were Nina's, her only sustenance for months. These arms also hers. They held her every day—she was a baby that never wanted to be put down, she was a child who gave long, intense hugs with her whole body. A koala, really. My arms grew stronger as she grew bigger and they carried her every day, until there was nobody left to carry. These are thoughts that strike and swirl for hours in the middle of the night. These are thoughts that pop in to say hello while I fold laundry or try to read a book.

Sometimes when she's at school, my mind goes to the playground, and I think how easy it would be for some psycho with an AR-15 to pick off a bunch of toddlers from the hill behind the parking lot. *I would cease to live*, I think. *I would shave my head and live out the rest of my days as a Buddhist nun. Or I would die from grief. Or I would find the shooter and kill them myself and die in a maximum-security prison from starvation.*

A walk through a cemetery with my child might naturally trigger these thoughts, my deepest fears, but somehow it does not affect Nina. A toddler lives nowhere but in the present moment; it's best when I can meet her there. *Just this* puddle. *Just this* finger tracing along an angel's face. *Just this. Just this. Just this.*

And then there's our dog Bowie who we must keep from marking the gravestones.

"Bowieeeeee, noooooo!" Nina yells, running headlong toward our little dog whose leg is poised to piss on the tallest monolith in this row of graves. "Oh my gaaawwd, Bowie," she says. "He's making Jesus cry."

"That's it, Bowie," I say. "Back on the leash."

Nina is leaping over graves so old they have sunken into the earth and she's singing a song I didn't teach her, or at least a version unknown to me. Her sneaker catches on the uneven ground and she falls to her hands and knees and stays there regarding muddy fingers. "You okay, bud? Can you get up on your own?" I ask. I'm not one to discourage dirty play, but I can't have her digging around in the graveyard mud, so I lift her by her armpits, swing her upright and kiss the damp top of her head. She smells like peanut butter and her lavender shampoo. Off she plods toward another puddle, wiping hands on the front of jacket, the sides of pants. It is starting to rain, and Jesus's face, angled just so, is sad and wet, and rain pools in the folds of his robe. I don't want my kid to fear death, I think to myself, but I also don't want her to grow up and not understand the conventions of faith and grieving.

Now she's rearranging the cob-webbed nylon flowers in another grave's built-in vase. I stop myself from stopping her. Who am I to squelch her curiosity, to censor these innocent gestures of care? I am uncomfortable with crucifixes. I am afraid of death. But she doesn't need to be, not yet, anyway. I notice a car approach and park nearby and I flush with embarrassment. It is an older couple getting out of the car, stooped and slow-moving. One carries a bouquet of yellow lilies, the other doffs his hat. They are here to remember someone. We are just killing time.

"Hey kiddo, how 'bout a cheese stick?"

"Yeah!" She says, grinning and bounding over grave markers toward my outstretched hand. We find a bench and sit, pulling cheese into long strings and whipping them into our mouths. Bowie is perched at our feet, begging. But for her swinging legs, Nina is still, contained, and we are safe here on this bench from the judgment— not of Jesus, Jesus still looms—but of the grieving couple. My hands and feet are numb again. Is it the cold air or something more sinister? Nina gives herself a cheese mustache and mugs for me. I scooch her closer to me so I can feel her warm, wiggly body. *I'm going to miss this*, I think. I blame the pandemic, the CT scans, the cemetery and all these engraved dates. Beginnings and ends.

My people are buried all over: A couple of grandparents in the veteran's cemetery in Augusta, another grandmother and an aunt at a family plot in Kennebunk's First Parish Church cemetery. My nana offered my parents a place in the ground next to her, but they demurred. We'll scatter my father's ashes from mountain tops and into rivers. My mom wants to be composted. "Where will I go to visit you?" I asked her after she told me her plans. She was weeding her veggie beds. "Nowhere. Everywhere? I'll just be part of the carbon cycle, dear," she said, handing me a warm, juicy sun-gold tomato, straight from the vine. I make a mental note to call my mother when the car is done. She's watching Nina tomorrow while I go to the doctor. *Thank God for my mother*, I think.

The cheese is gone and so are the bereaved. Our car won't be ready for another half hour at least and I sense a lull in Nina's enchantment with this place. She's starting to whine about her dirty, wet pants and I don't have a change of clothes. The dog shivers and is looking at me like *What the fuck are we doing here?* I wish we were home, but to say so would only invite the possibility of misery. Here is where a parent must reach deep and perform. I pop up from the bench, stick my butt way out behind me, flap my elbows like a speed-walking chicken and holler over my shoulder:

"Hey Nina, would you still love me if I walked like this?"

The dog lopes after me, his leash dragging, and Nina follows, her giggle in a low tenuous register.

"Ha, ha, no way, Mama. That's ridiculous!"

Now she's stuttering on tippy toes, her hands look like they're playing the piano and her head bobs forward and back like a pigeon. "Would you love me if I walked like *this?*"

"Oh yeah, I'd love you. I would love you no matter how silly you walk."

"I would, too. I'd love you even if you walked like *this*!" she says. Her knees bend and her legs cross as she hops forward, her arms swing for momentum and balance and her tongue curls up over her top lip the way mine does when I'm concentrating.

"Wow. You love me a lot," I say. "But what if I walked like this?"

And on and on it goes, the silly walks, the declarations of unconditional love. This time is all ours, and we are alive, stomping through puddles and leaping over graves. We are audaciously alive. And I'm sorry, dearly departed, to flaunt it, but I suppose I'm grateful for the distraction in the presence of so much stillness.

The dog's whole underside is mud. Nina has started practicing her cartwheels on a wet grassy patch when my phone buzzes. It's the garage calling to say our car is ready.

"Wahoo! The car is ready. Let's head back. Boogie, boogie. Boogie on, Nina."

"Boogie on, Mama!" she calls over her shoulder as she silly runs back toward the cemetery gate and the four-lane highway.

"Boogie on, Bowie," I say to our stalwart companion, trotting alongside me.

"Boogie on, Jesus," says Nina, looking up as we pass the crucifix in the middle of the graveyard. It's still crying.

"Boogie on, Jesus!" I echo, laughing.

We're both laughing now, tight belly laughs, and we're crying we're laughing so hard. I love that raspy, puckish laugh of hers, and she loves making me laugh so she keeps saying it. "Boogie on, Jesus. Boogie on." We hold hands as we pass through the wrought iron gate and make our way back across the busy four-lane highway.

AMIRITE

LUKE JOHNSON

For you, my love, I swallow
this knife. & if not this knife
a bushel of swallows,
who slap the hood while I pin
the pedal, free hand floating
the smog. But what of pillows
with kept creases,
the shoes left scattered, the socks?
Silent mothers? For you, an apple pie. For you,
the bodies of boys: my body, any
body, anyone. A gown of goat necks
& boat strung with bonnets, a violent sky
violet with rain. Forget me. I too
have tasted spider silk & woven
a home from shrapnel & sea glass, strut
like a muscular god. For you, this foolish weather. The white
noise, the willows, the winnowing fog. For you,
this anguish, its pewter stench. Ten thousand
tongues & the bombs who torched them. For you,
their buried swell.

HOW TO DIE

KALILA HOLT

I'd only written the story because Mr. Henry had given this big speech about how we were "freewriting," and how freewriting meant we shouldn't censor or judge ourselves. I didn't realize that freewriting also meant reading your unjudged work aloud to the whole class. I think I was hoping that maybe if I read quietly enough, no one would understand what I was saying. But people did understand.

"How to Die," I read. "Step one. Come up with a reason why you absolutely can't go on. This can be anything—maybe your boyfriend broke up with you, or you didn't get into your dream school. If you can't think of a reason, that's okay. Don't leave a note and people will read their own deep reason into it."

Lots of kids laughed, even the popular boys who never looked at me. Mr. Henry clapped his hands together and went, "Great!" But other kids looked down at their desks uncomfortably. These were the kids who knew Hannah.

"This is special," Mr. Henry told me when I stayed after class to tell him I'd made a huge mistake. "I really think you should keep working on this as your final project. Lean into the taboo."

I didn't know how to explain to him. Mr. Henry had very blue eyes and wore band T-shirts and made jokes about celebrity gossip. All the girls had crushes on him. This was the longest conversation we'd ever had. "Okay," I said, and went to math class, where we were working on an unlikely hypothetical scenario about planting a circular orchard. All through class, I could feel the story contaminating my backpack. I wanted to burn it. I wanted to have never written it. I had two more pages due by Friday.

My mom picked me up after school, because it was a day where her shift ended early at the salon. It was actually her first day back at work since everything had happened. I, on the other hand, had not missed even a single day of school, even though she'd wanted me to.

I asked my mom how work went, and she said, "Fine." She asked me how school went, and I said, "Fine." I waited for her to say something else, but she didn't, so I didn't either. I looked out the window at a series of signs someone had put along their cornfield. "In despair?" said one. "Jesus offers hope," said the next. Then the last one promised that Jesus was on his way back here.

The phone rang as we walked into the house, and my mom grabbed it on the first ring, all panicked. Since Hannah had come home from the hospital, my mom had been very worried about there being too much noise. She made us watch TV with the volume down low, even though as far as I knew, Hannah had never *asked* for absolute silence.

"It's for you," my mom told me, sounding annoyed, I guess because the additional decibels infiltrating the house had now become my responsibility.

"It's Kinsley," said Kinsley on the phone.

"I figured," I said. Kinsley was my best friend. No one else ever called me.

"I think I have a new crush," said Kinsley.

"Who?" I asked.

"You have to guess!" said Kinsley.

"Is it someone in our grade?" I asked.

"Yes," said Kinsley.

"Mia, keep your voice down," said my mom.

"I'm not even talking loud," I said.

"You're practically *shouting*," said my mom.

I asked Kinsley if I could come do my homework at her house. She said sure.

Step two: Decide how much you really want to die. This will affect which method you choose. If you think you might not want to die, and are more interested in people hugging you and saying how much they love you and bringing you desserts in your room while you recover, it is best to choose a method that will probably fail. Plan your death for when someone will be coming home. Take some pills, but not enough. However, if you're sure you want to die, then you must choose a method that is foolproof. You must plan carefully, and you must not flinch.

Kinsley's new crush was Stephen Lapore, who was a jockish freshman in my creative writing class. I thought he was a little boring, but this was Kinsley's type—beautiful and simple. Now Kinsley and I were sitting on her bedroom floor eating cold Pop-Tarts, and I was trying to get more of my stupid story written. I wrote a long paragraph about carbon monoxide poisoning and then crossed the whole thing out.

"Do you think I could sleep over?" I asked Kinsley.

"I dunno," she said. "My mom just gave me a whole lecture about sleepovers on weeknights. She like, cut out all these articles about how important sleep is to the developing brain."

"Oh, okay," I said.

"Hey, will you look at this?" asked Kinsley, and held up her geometry homework.

"Sure," I said, and scooted towards her. I'd passed out of geometry. She'd been going about the problem all wrong. I wrote a few things down.

"Wow," she said, taking her paper back. "Thank you. How's it feel to be a genius?"

"Shut up," I said.

I liked Kinsley's room. It felt peaceful, with big windows and a canopy bed and a white writing desk. My room felt cramped by comparison—Hannah, as the oldest, had gotten the bigger one. Kinsley and I used to debate who was luckier. I thought she was, because as an only child, she wasn't fighting for resources. She thought I was, because I had a way to diffuse the pressure on me and I also got Hannah as a friend. Of course, this was before what had happened. Now we did not debate who was luckier. We did not talk about my house or my mom or Hannah at all.

Kinsley had come to the hospital right after, along with everyone else—she'd brought Hannah a teddy bear. I wasn't sure what had happened to the bear, ultimately. I knew they wouldn't let Hannah have many things in there.

"You could probably stay for dinner," Kinsley offered. "My mom's making a lasagna."

Step three: Prepare. Gather the necessary materials. Depending on your method, you may not need any materials at all. If you have unfinished business, now is the time to finish it. Say the things you need to say. Return any videotapes or jackets you may have borrowed. But do this casually. Say, "Oh, I realized I still have this," or the like. Otherwise, people may catch on. You may decide to write letters to leave behind, but they probably won't come out the way you want them to.

Next class, we had to read aloud again. I should have anticipated this, probably, but I hadn't. Even though a lot of people laughed again, Taylor Prise made this face like I was waving a Nazi flag. She caught up with me afterwards in the hallway. "Hey!" she said.

"Hi," I said. I didn't know Taylor at all. She was a junior. Her and Hannah had been on the soccer team together. I'd heard a rumor that she'd kissed a teacher. That was all I knew.

"I think what you're writing is really morbid and messed up," she said. Then she raised her eyebrows at me and walked away before I could say anything.

I ducked into a bathroom stall and put my head between my knees. The soccer team had sent Hannah a card they all signed. I couldn't remember what Taylor had written on it—probably something like, "Feel better!" I was pretty sure the card had been the coach's idea. Hannah usually went to the library at lunch, rather than sitting with the soccer girls. She didn't go to their parties or lean against their lockers to talk.

I wished I could throw up, to expel some of the feeling in my chest. But I couldn't, and the feeling just sat there. Around me, toilets flushed, girls screeched with laughter, and then an abrupt hush fell as class started. I ended up being five minutes late to trig, but it was the first time I'd ever been late in my entire life and so the teacher didn't say anything.

I was getting this stupid prize for academic leaders called the James Whitting Award. There was going to be a ceremony at a school assembly. I didn't really get anything for it, aside from a certificate and a bunch of people looking at me. I was the only freshman to receive this award.

"Here," I told my mom. "They told me to give you this form." The form was to invite her to the ceremony.

My mom was making up a tray for Hannah. It had a sandwich and a glass of milk, even though I'd never seen Hannah drink milk before. Now she was arranging some dandelions in a tiny vase. "Did you pick those from the yard?" I asked her.

"Bring this up to your sister, please," said my mom.

I could feel the room start to float around me. I had not actually looked at Hannah since she'd returned from the hospital. "Mom, did you hear me about the form?"

"What?" she said, glancing down at the form without really reading it. "Yes, thank you, I see it." She nodded at the tray. "Take that up to Hannah," she repeated.

"I can't right now," I said.

"Mia," she said. "Why are you making my life difficult?"

That was a joke—that *I* was the one making her life difficult. "I have a ton of homework," I said. "And I told Kinsley I'd help her with hers."

"It'll take thirty seconds."

"Then why can't you just do it?"

"This is not up for discussion," she said, and walked out of the room.

I stared at the tray. A fly was buzzing around the sandwich. I waved it away. I wondered what would happen if I just left the tray there and went to do something else. I wasn't sure how long it took for milk to go bad sitting out like that. The fly was back. I waved it away again. I didn't like the idea of Hannah eating a sandwich that a fly had been on. I picked up the tray and walked upstairs.

Hannah's room was at the end of the hall. Creeping over there gave me the same feeling as trying to go kill a centipede. But I didn't think of my sister as a bug and even making the comparison made me feel like a bad person. I took another step forward and the floor gave a loud creak. I was sure Hannah had heard it.

"Hannah?" I called. I didn't like how weak my voice sounded. "Can I come in?"

"Mm," said Hannah.

"It's Mia," I added, like she might be confused. Her door was closed, and I had to set down the tray to open it.

Hannah still had all the curtains closed and the lights off. The air was stale and smelled vaguely metallic, like a messy period. She had the blanket pulled up to her eyes. Her hair was a dark nest on the pillow. I thought her eyes looked kind of strange, sunken, like a skull. Her skull, I guess.

"Here you go! I said. "Mom put milk on it for some reason."

I tried to set the tray down fast on her lap and it almost fell over, sloshing milk and dislodging a pickle from the sandwich. "I'll put it on the floor here," I said. I couldn't tell if she was listening to me. I was afraid she might try and say something.

"Okay, bye, Hannah!" I said. I closed the door and sprinted downstairs.

The next morning, as I was leaving for school, I noticed there was a coffee ring on the James Whitting Award form.

This new version of Hannah was not like the old one. The old Hannah would sit with me on the couch till three a.m., shit talking. The old Hannah went with me to buy my first bra. The old Hannah was the one who, when our dad left and I was too young to under-stand, dragged her mattress into my room and slept on my floor. The old Hannah liked things—highlighters in different colors, Sprite,

Mia Hamm. The old Hannah was sad too, I guess, but I felt that I could help. I was good at giving the old Hannah advice, and before long we'd be back to putting string cheese in the microwave or taking a quiz to see at what age we'd get married.

The new Hannah was not like this. The new Hannah was honestly kind of annoying. The new Hannah would complain that she couldn't motivate herself to do her homework, and I'd say, "Well, the only way is to just get started," and she would say, "I can't," and I would say, "You have to, just do it," and she would start watching TV, and I would say, "Do you want me to do it for you?" and she would say, "I'm not an idiot, Mia," and then she would say what was the point, anyway, in homework, why were we doing it at all? And I would say, "So we can learn," and she would go to her room. The new Hannah started going to doctors who gave her pills, pills that made her nauseous so that then she started taking different pills, until she said those pills weren't doing anything and so she started different pills. The new Hannah would take hours in the bathroom when I needed to be getting ready and then come out looking the same. The new Hannah would snap at me when I finished the box of Honey Nut Cheerios and then write a Xanga post about how no one really cared about her. These posts always got a lot of comments. "We love you, girl!" they said. "We're here for you!" Although, I'd like to note, it's not like any of those commenters had been stopping by our house lately.

The day before, the new Hannah had sat next to me on the couch while I was eating popcorn and doing trig and said, "I really don't think I can do this anymore." She said stuff like that all the time, though.

"You have to," I said, and then went back to my homework.

Step four: This is death itself. I cannot help you here. You must go alone, as we all do.

At lunch, Stephen Lapore walked up to us and said, "Hey."

"Mm," said Kinsley. Her eyes were wide and her mouth was full of cafeteria chicken fingers.

"Can we sit here?" asked Stephen. He was with a friend who basically looked the same as him, only wearing a different colored hat.

"Uh," said Kinsley.

"Of course," I said, to save Kinsley from herself.

Stephen introduced himself to Kinsley. "Yeah, we have math together," said Kinsley.

"Oh, what's your name again?" asked Stephen.

"Kinsley. We also have bio together."

"This is my buddy Leo," said Stephen.

"Yo," said Leo.

"We're in the same gym class, too," said Kinsley. I kicked her.

"I'm Mia," I said.

"Mia's in my creative writing class," Stephen told Leo, his teeth tearing into chicken flesh. "She's writing this really funny shit right now."

"You are?" asked Kinsley.

"Not really," I said.

"Dude, this shit is *hilarious*," said Stephen. He started laughing just thinking about it. "It's like a guide on how to kill yourself."

"Tight," said Leo.

Kinsley snapped her head to look at me. "You're writing that?"

I shrugged and took a big bite of my chocolate chip cookie. But it was like my mouth was suddenly too dry to eat anything. I kept chewing and chewing and chewing.

"So what sports do you guys play?" I asked, when I'd mostly swallowed.

"What?" laughed Leo.

"Football, basketball," said Stephen.

"Soccer," chimed in Kinsley, but it seemed like her heart wasn't in it.

Somehow Leo and Stephen had already finished their entire lunches, even draining their chocolate milks and crushing the cartons. By comparison, Kinsley and I had made virtually no progress at all. "Well, later," said Stephen, and they walked away in a cloud of swagger and Axe body spray.

"I think you came off a little desperate," I told Kinsley. It sounded meaner than I'd intended.

"Mia," said Kinsley. "Are you really writing that?"

I'm the one who found her. She had to know I would—my mom always had to work late on Wednesdays. Hannah had stayed home sick that day, but she'd waited to do it until right before I got home from school. I don't know what would have happened if I'd gotten caught up talking to Kinsley or something—if I'd been running late.

It had been a good day. It was unseasonably warm outside. My advisory teacher had told me I'd be getting the James Whitting Award. I knew it didn't mean anything, but still, I was proud. Walking home, I'd seen a cardinal sitting on a fence.

She'd left the bathroom door unlocked, and after knocking for a while and complaining that I had to pee, I walked in. She was in the bathtub but, bizarrely, wearing a swimsuit. I guess she didn't want to be taken to the hospital naked. It took me several seconds to even process what I was looking at. For some reason, when I walked in, I'd thought, "Oh, she got some sort of food all over her arms." I still had to pee, and I have to admit that, after I called the ambulance, I did. I could hear the sirens approaching. Hannah wasn't moving at all.

I didn't like to walk in that room anymore. There was one tile that still looked discolored, that I guess my mom hadn't been able to get clean. Unfortunately, the bathroom is the one room that is impossible to avoid.

Step five: If you've made it this far, then you've failed. Congratulations, or I'm sorry, as the case may be.

"Does Hannah know you're writing that?" Kinsley asked me. Lunch was over and we were walking to class. I'd tried to distract her with questions like, had she noticed Stephen Lapore's sweatshirt? Did she need me to look at her geometry homework? But for once, Kinsley was impossible to distract. She was walking around with her hands clutched, giving me a look like I was suffering dementia.

"Hannah just sits in the dark all day," I said. "She doesn't care what I do."

TAHOMA LITERARY REVIEW 39

"Hannah loves you, Mia," said Kinsley.

I rolled my eyes. What did Kinsley know? She didn't have any siblings and she certainly didn't have Hannah as a sibling. The warning bell rang. "I have to get to Spanish," I told her.

"I think Hannah would be really hurt to find out you were writing that."

"I think Hannah has bigger problems than my creative writing homework."

"You don't actually think suicide is funny, do you? Because I've been doing some research, and it's one of the biggest problems facing teens today."

"Shut *up*, Kinsley, my god!"

She clamped her mouth closed and her face got red. It was impossible to yell at Kinsley. It was like beating a puppy. "I'm sorry," I said instantly, and gave her a hug. She clutched me back. She smelled like Herbal Essences. "I was an accident," I said. "I don't know. It just happened."

"Out of the way, lesbos!" some upperclassman shouted. This was because we were blocking the flow of foot traffic. We let go of each other.

During Spanish class, the secretary Ms. Wood tiptoed in and said I needed to come to the office.

"Oooh!" said everyone.

"Silencio!" said Señor Cabrera. We were supposed to only be speaking Spanish. I wondered if you said "oooh" differently.

Ms. Wood's high heels clacked loudly in the empty hall. I'd never been called to the office before. It was really more of a Hannah thing. "They're all ready for you," said Ms. Wood, and smiled. She had lipstick on her tooth. I didn't know who "they all" was, but I followed the direction her hand was gesturing.

Dr. Davidson, the principal, was sitting behind his big desk in a suit. Behind him on the left was Mr. Henry, who was wearing an Arctic Monkeys T-shirt and staring at his hands. On the right was a mousy woman who Dr. Davidson said was the guidance counselor. I didn't even know we had a guidance counselor.

"Sit down," Dr. Davidson suggested, because I'd been standing there, frozen. I sat down, although I didn't want to. It made them all suddenly taller than me.

"Do you know why you're here?" asked Dr. Davidson.

"My story?" I guessed.

"We understand you've been working on some troubling material."

"Mr. Henry told me to continue," I said, although I felt weak throwing him under the bus so quickly.

"That was my mistake, Mia," said Mr. Henry, looking up suddenly. "I didn't understand the backstory." He flashed me a tight smile.

"He didn't realize it was so personal to your family," Dr. Davidson clarified.

"So it's only okay to write about things you *don't* know anything about?" I'd never taken a tone like that with a teacher before, but I was suddenly mad. It didn't seem fair that someone like Stephen Lapore could write about suicide and it would be no problem because no one in his family had ever decided to die.

"Mia," said the woman who was supposedly the guidance counselor. Her voice sounded creaky, like she was using it for the first time in several years. "We just want to talk to you. We want to make sure you have the support you need."

"How are you supporting me? By making me miss Spanish class?"

"It's natural to act out when you're working through something troubling."

"I literally don't even understand how I acted out. I did my assignment. I listened to my teacher. I turned it in on time." I scratched my hand too hard. It left a red line on my skin.

"Mia, surely you understand that it's the subject matter that's the issue here," said Dr. Davidson.

"Okay, so you *don't* want me to talk about it? Or you do?"

"There's a time and a place to talk about it," said Dr. Davidson. "To write about it in class like that, some of the other students found it disturbing."

"Oh," I said, rolling my eyes. "I'm so sorry. I'm so sorry if I *disturbed* anyone. That must have been awful for them."

"Mia," said the guidance counselor. Everyone kept saying my name. "Have you been having any suicidal thoughts?"

"No," I said.

"It's okay, you can tell me."

"I'm not lying," I said. "I'm not selfish like that."

"Do you think of your sister as selfish?" asked the guidance counselor.

"Do I have to be here?" I asked. "I mean, is there more you have to say to me or can I go back to class?"

"We want to provide you with a safe space to talk," said the guidance counselor.

"Thank you, but I'm good," I said.

"And you do need to know that we can't allow this kind of behavior," piped in Dr. Davidson.

"I didn't do anything!" I said. My nose was starting to drip. I needed to get out of the room. I needed to get to the bathroom and wipe my nose and splash water on my face and I need to get back to Spanish before Señor Cabrera explained what the homework was. I picked up my backpack and turned to leave.

"Mia," said Dr. Davidson.

But Mr. Henry said, "Clark, let her go." All those girls were right, it turned out, about Mr. Henry being so great.

It was a Wednesday, so I had to walk home. I wondered if I needed to write some sort of apology to the administration. I wondered if they'd take away my award. I walked past a cornfield, passing those signs about God, but more slowly since I was on foot. "In despair?" A car full of guys honked at me—I wasn't sure why, but it can't have been for anything good. "Jesus offers hope."

At home, the air was still and silent. I walked upstairs.

"Hannah?" I called. "Can I come in?" I couldn't hear anything inside, and I felt my adrenaline spike—what if she was really dead this time?

But then she went, "Okay."

She looked a little better than the last time I'd come up. She was still wearing her pajamas, but she was sitting up cross-legged on the bed. It looked like she'd washed her hair. Her wrists were still bandaged. I stood in the doorway, staring at her.

"Are you gonna like, sit down?" asked Hannah.

"Yes," I said, and perched on the edge of the mattress. "It's like, really dark in here."

"I like it," said Hannah.

"It's depressing," I said.

"It's peaceful," said Hannah.

Hannah had an old poster on her wall for the movie *Bend It Like Beckham*. One corner was hanging down, blocking Kiera Knightley's face. "Isn't Mom freaked out about leaving you all day?" I asked.

"Yeah," snorted Hannah. "She calls me every hour. She also hid a bunch of stuff but I'm sure it's in her closet."

"Yeah," I agreed. It was where our mom hid everything. "When do you think you'll go back to school again?"

"They're still figuring that out," said Hannah. "It's going to be a shit show."

I didn't know what to say. I wanted to apologize for writing what I had, but I also didn't want Hannah to know that I'd written it at all. I wanted Hannah to apologize to me. I wanted to hit her. I wanted to hug her. I wanted her to tell me it would never happen again.

"You'll be okay," I told her. I knew this was the thing I was supposed to believe.

NEON HYMN: Excerpt
KONSTANTIN KULAKOV

I.

Money is Winter

The Zaoksky boys put their hands on my polo—and thinking I may
fall—I stepped from my bike. I stood in the mud. *Majzor, majzor,*
they shouted. They asked me: *what's that on your neck? Binoculars*
I answered. I thought they wanted what I had, a gift from my dad,
"the pastor in Oxford." *Majzor, majzor* jealously.

They pull at my polo, shouting *majzor, majzor.* So muddy. They do
not know that—soon—in Carolina, preps will laugh at my polo.
The preps will tell me it is fake lacoste; they will say *did you steal it
from your sister?* I will labor to be a prep—not *majzor*—because the
preps sit in the smart classes and their parent's cars.

The boys in Zaoksky do not know that in America, a church lady
will take me to her grandad's farm and point to muddy land: *that's
where they buried the slaves; they were good ones.* The Z-boys do not
know between prep nor majzor. No one walks the air.

In America, I will be white, churched: whiteboyjeezus like money is
winter.

II.

The Call

defect   pastor son thrown out

by church and tavern   baptized

by lake water, churched by city   cyrillic

confuses my english   whiteness en-

forces   masks   skins   moneys   kills

the world

here on this fire escape

holding out for an impossible candor

(with you) listening among neon hymns—

III.

Vow

grandpa, this house is more wound than home. grandpa, your cover
job was photography. grandpa, memory hurts. it is christmas, russia
& we are holding plastic cups in front of tree glitter. grandpa, in the
home video you talk eternity & say this feast is a taste of the feast to
come. grandpa, under nightcover, you baptized in the lake. by the
fanta you talk bread crumbs in prison pockets & across the atlantic,
now it's the 90s housing boom. grandpa, i think you have more
in common with mumia abu-jamal & antonio gramsci than billy
graham & robert pierson. more than one of your sons is still upset
with you & when he caught you bowed in prayer, he said you bowed
like there was a presence in the room. after gulags it was courts &
kazakstan. dedushka, i preach & don't go to church. church is where
people suffer together. dedushka, it is in your paint brushes & psalms
too, *you* know eternity is not shaped from drywall. dedushka, carrying
a cup, i was not thinking, but bowed to the ground. i presented
myself penitent & i wasn't thinking & i bowed, a cup between palms.
дедушка, i am running into harm's way. i hear the hymn in the neon,
crackling. i see the neon humming in the birch grove. дедушка:
behind this supper the feast to come behind all this color the light.

What They Don't Teach You in Catholic School
Amber Blaeser-Wardzala

Someone handed you a toothbrush and told you to brush. Someone handed you a Q-tip and told you to twist. Someone handed you a Kleenex and told you to blow. No one ever handed you Vagisil and told you to scrub. It's common sense, you suppose, but it never crossed your mind to wash down there, to spread your legs in the shower and take handfuls of water and toss it up, rinse it out. It's another hole, and you have to clean all your other holes, but you never thought to clean that one with anything more than toilet paper.

You're watching a YouTube makeup tutorial. The woman chats about her life as she does her eyeshadow. Usually you watch the videos on mute. You're not sure why you have the volume on. The woman mentions she recently stopped using soap to clean her vagina, that she's only using water. She says she likes that better, that it feels better that way.

You stop in your attempt to replicate her blue smokey eye, your brush in your crease, blue powder falling onto your high cheekbones. You turn the volume up, use your thumbs to press your earbuds in further so you make sure you hear her correctly over the noise of your roommate's phone call. You rewind the video and listen to her say those words again. You listen to her talk about cleaning her vagina. You look over to your roommate. She sits on her bed, looking towards the window as she twists some of her black hair around her finger and laughs. You wonder if she knows this. You wonder if someone in her life told her to clean it or if she was smart enough to figure it out on her own.

You feel like a failure, like you're fulfilling the stereotype of the "filthy Indian savage." A completely unfounded stereotype to begin with. Your people taught the white men how to bath, not the other way around. Maybe that's the issue. Maybe it's the white in your biracial identity. Maybe your Polish ancestors are the ones who didn't know how to clean their vaginas.

You never learned the female reproductive system. In high school health class, your teacher quits two weeks into the semester. Or maybe he's fired. When you ask your religion teacher what happened to him, she changes the subject to the weather, how she hopes the humidity gives way to a fall breeze soon.

They hire a sub. He's old enough to be your grandfather. He brings in his newspaper and reads it aloud to you. He gives you quizzes on the news. He tells you jokes that are thinly veiled stories about his marriage to his wife who probably doesn't love him. He tells the class you can do anything as long as you don't start a riot. He never teaches anything health-related. He ends each class with, "Don't do drugs; stay in school."

They hire a real, full-time health teacher with only a month left in the semester. She crams in as much material as she can. You learn about the penis, the testicles, the prostrate, the seminal vesicle, the epididymis, the scrotum. You even memorize their spelling for the quiz, because the teacher tells you she won't give you the points if you don't spell them right. During review, she misspells "epididymis" as "epediymiss." You ask her why you need to know how to spell them if she doesn't even know how to.

She never teaches you the female anatomy.

You're twenty when you first hear the word clitoris. You're playing Cards Against Humanity. The other girls laugh when you read the card aloud. In general, they know you have a dirty sense of humor. They expect you to laugh. You should have faked it and chosen that card as the winner so you could google its meaning in secret later. But you don't realize it's a dirty joke. You think a clitoris is some white person thing you've never heard of. There's a lot of white people things you don't know about—this wouldn't be the first. You ask them what it is.

Sometimes at night, the looks on their faces return to you. You'll never wish you could unsay words as much as you wish you could unsay those.

The first time you came was an accident. You weren't even touching yourself. You were watching an R-rated movie on your laptop in your room. Your parents had gone to bed, but you were still worried about being caught—by them or by your brother across the hallway. You aren't old enough to watch an R-movie yet. Your brother would definitely tell.

You watch it in the dark, the screen brightness as low as it can go so no light will escape under the crack of your door and alert people to your misdeed. You have the subtitles on, because you have it going so quietly you can barely hear anything. Your cat sleeps at the end of your bed.

You don't even remember what movie it was. You don't even remember the plot or who the actors are. None of that matters. It wasn't their faces you were looking at.

You do remember the full frontal. It's the first penis you've seen.

The naked man in the movie takes the woman in his arms and kisses her. You can see their tongues teasing each other. You lean forward, getting close to the screen so you can see everything. He tosses her on the bed and climbs on top. You squeeze your legs together, press them as hard as you can against one other. It cuts to the actors' shadows, and you see the shadows becoming one, see his thrusting in. Even with the volume on low, you hear the woman's moan. Or maybe it's your own moan.

That's when you lose control of your muscles, your abdomen spasming, your butt raising off the bed, your mouth forming an O, and this time you know the sounds are your own. You try to stop them, to quench them, because if you shouldn't be caught watching an R-rated movie, you know you can't be caught doing whatever it is your body is doing. You can't keep the sounds in, just like you can't stop the way your body moves, can't stop the pleasure that is washing through you.

You snap your laptop shut the moment you regain control of your body. You don't watch the end of the film. You guess you'll never see it.

You don't know what just happened, you don't know what that was. They never taught you anything about that in Family Life class at your Catholic middle school. You lie back on the bed, close your eyes, and bask in the warmth, the leftover pleasure. You don't understand what your body did. But you liked it. Whatever it was you liked it very much, and that's what scares you the most. Usually, the things you like aren't good for you—like potato chips or riding your bike with no helmet or staying up until three a.m. You think you did something you weren't supposed to. You feel like your body did something wrong. You think there's something wrong with you.

You open your eyes. Your cat is awake now. Her green eyes stare at you. They watch you, judge you through the darkness. She saw it all. You can't see anything but her eyes, can't make out the shape of her in the dark. Only her watching eyes. The longer you look into them, the worse you feel about what happened.

You don't have a word for it for three more years. Even then, you don't know it's something that can happen to women. You think only people with penises can come. You know only that it happens to make a baby.

It's another two years before you know that word can apply to you too.

After that first time, you don't come again for eight years. You want to. Even before you know what to call it, you want to feel that again, to experience the tendrils of bliss across your skin, inside your being. But every time you get close, you remember your cat's eyes, the way they condemned you. You remember thinking pleasure like that isn't something you should have, isn't something you deserve.

Even now, it takes you a long time to come. Your mind tells you it's wrong, it's wrong, you're wrong. You shouldn't be doing what you're doing. What would your parents think if they knew you were doing this? What would God think—even though you don't believe in him anymore but theoretically if he does happen to be real and is watching you, what would he think? He would tell you that's not what he made your body for. Didn't you pay attention during those thirteen years of Catholic school? Didn't you learn that your body was created to serve God and please your future husband? Your body was never yours to use like this. It's a sin. It's a sin. It's a fucking sin, and you need to stop it right now or you'll be banished to hell to live among other greedy women who used their bodies for things they were never intended to do.

You need a lot of foreplay to turn off your brain. And he obliges, doesn't complain about all the time he spends rubbing your clit, sucking on your nipples, kissing your neck. He wants you to get there too. He puts in all the work before you move onto the actual sex part. He rarely rushes the process. But sometimes, even after all of that, as you're approaching the peak, your mind will whisper *you fucking redskin slut.* You hear the words in the voice of someone from your high school. Behind your closed eyelids, you see the curl of their mouth, the spit on their bottom lip as they call you that name. You never make it to the peak, never make it over the edge to orgasm. It's as if you're rock climbing and as you reach up for that last rock, the last hold to pull you up onto the cliff's edge, you slip and lose your hold and go cascading back to the ground to start all over again. All those sounds you were making as you felt it coming, all the movements your body made against his, were lies, nothing more than red herrings.

Sometimes you fake it, to make you and him feel better, to make yourself feel less broken, less of a burden to him. He never figures out. You always did want to be an actress.

You have a panic attack the first time you try to finger yourself. You're claustrophobic. Deeply so. Who knew you could be claustrophobic down there too?

You heard some of the other girls talking about fingering themselves at your club soccer practice. You're on the outskirts of the team, talk little to anyone because you don't think you're a good enough player to actually be on the team and you think if you draw too much attention to yourself, they'll kick you off. The other girls rarely notice you hovering along their edges, listening to their conversations.

It's a few days before your period, and your body is screaming, screaming for something to be inside of you. You set your cat in the hallway outside your room, lock your door, and turn off the horse lamp next to your bed. You slide your fingers between your legs. You can't find the opening. You turn the lamp back on and grab your green makeup mirror. You crawl back into bed, hold the mirror between your legs with your left hand. It takes you several tries before you find the opening. It's so wet. You're so wet. You slid one finger in and sit with the feeling. You set the mirror on the nightstand before sliding a second finger in.

You hate it. There's a sense of relief, having something in you, but you hate it. The feeling of the walls of your vagina closing in around your fingers is awful. You keep them there, move them slowly in and out, curl the tips gently. You feel no pleasure beyond that initial relief, because you're worrying you won't be able to get your fingers out. You worry the vagina hole will shrink and your fingers will be stuck there and then you'll have to call 911 with your other hand and the ambulance will come and take you to the emergency room and the doctors will debate what to do and as they debate, the walls of your vagina will continue to close in around your fingers, turning them blue, and you'll scream, *Cut them off, just cut them off!* and the doctors won't know what else to do—this hasn't happened before, they didn't learn about this at their third-tier med schools— so they do and they'll cut off the two fingers stuck inside of you, and they'll just leave them there and tell you they'll pass through you in seven years like gum and they'll stitch up your nubs and send you home eight-fingered instead of ten-fingered and your parents won't look at you or say anything on the fifteen-minute drive home—a taste of your future because no one will ever be able to look at you again without seeing your missing fingers and knowing the other two are inside of you still, waiting for the seven years to pass so they can fall out and you'll be a perfect example at your Catholic school when they teach about the punishments of masturbation.

You rip your fingers out. Spots dance across your vision as you struggle to breath. You rock back and forth on the bed, back and forth. The squeaking of the springs makes it sound like you're doing something else. You stop and try to breath. You look to your nightstand. Your reflection stares back at you. You look away the moment you make eye contact.

You try fingering yourself two more times that month. You have a panic attack each time. You give up trying.

The first time someone else fingers you, you throw up. You don't do it until after he leaves. Can you imagine? He'd never touch you again.

You fake your enjoyment. It hurts. He goes too fast, and his nails are too long. He's eager to please, eager to make you feel good. You like that about him. You like that he wants you to feel good. You like that not everything is about him.

You worry telling him you don't like what he's doing will hurt his feelings. You worry asking him to be gentler will take away his enjoyment of it and he'll never try again. You've already ruined him touching your inner thighs with your thin line between turned-on and ticklish. You don't want to ruin this too. So instead, you moan and groan. You dig your nails into his back. You leave crescent-shaped indentations in his skin. He kisses your neck. He whispers how fucking gorgeous you are. You can't say any words. You worry if you try to, you'll start to cry.

It is a brief encounter, because he has an appointment in an hour and he wants to go home and change first and you're meeting a friend to go shopping in two hours. With his fingers still in you, your bodies curled around each other on the couch, he suggests you both cancel your plans. You pretend like you want that, but tell him you can't. He's disappointed.

At the door, you kiss him goodbye. He says he'll see you soon. He lingers with his hands on your butt, holding you to him. He's hard against you. You pretend not to notice.

You've barely shut the door before you're running to the bathroom to throw up. You feel a little better. The cramping he caused eases a little. You throw up two more times before you leave for your shopping trip. You wonder if anyone else has ever thrown up from being fingered.

Your friend asks you if you're feeling okay. She says you look ashy. You lie, tell her you're about to start your period and you're having bad cramps. At least the second part isn't a complete lie.

The first time you have sex you bleed for three days straight. You don't think that's normal, but how are you supposed to know? No one ever taught you how sex works. There was no article in the substitute health teacher's newspaper about the mechanics of sex. And when they hired the new health teacher, she only gave you an abstinence talk and told you condoms are a sin because they prevent God's miracles from being created.

There's no one you can ask—no one you want to ask anyways. You think everyone in your life will either judge you for having been a virgin or for no longer being a virgin. You don't want to endure either.

You worry you're going to die. The morning of your third day of bleeding while you sit in your car before heading to your morning shift, you try googling "is it bad I've been bleeding for three days straight after having sex for the first time" but all that comes up are articles talking about how a little blood your first time is normal. You wonder how much "a little" is. You think of the condom painted red. You think about the panty liners you have to change every couple of hours because you're out of pads and tampons hurt. You wonder how long the bleeding is supposed to last. You close the search tab and drive to work. That shift, you chew on your lower lip until it's bleeding too.

You can't ask him. You can't tell him. He doesn't know you were a virgin. You were worried he wouldn't want you if you told him. There was one brief moment early on in the relationship where you could have told him, but you only had five seconds to decide what to do and you chose to lie about it, because other men had already rejected you when they'd found out, and you didn't want that to happen again. If you told him now, after the fact, you think he would be weird about it. You don't know how he would react. Would he be mad that you lied? Would he feel betrayed or confused or wouldn't he care at all?

You wonder how he didn't know. You were so nervous and it took him forever to get his penis inside you because you were just that tight. Men aren't always the smartest—especially when they've been waiting nearly two months to get inside you. Or maybe he knows and he doesn't want to embarrass you by telling you he figured it out. Maybe he realized it as he struggled to get himself all the way in you, but he was too horny to really care if you were or weren't a virgin. And when he finished and saw the blood on the condom and on his stomach and on your thighs and you told him your period must have started and he said that's okay, that he doesn't mind, maybe he actually meant he doesn't mind you lying to him, doesn't mind that you were a virgin.

Who knows? Either way, you can't ask him if you should be concerned you still haven't stopped bleeding.

You wonder briefly if it is your period, but you know it's not. You're on birth control, and you're five days out from starting the placebo week, and you haven't been more than three minutes late taking your pill.

The day after your first time, you have sex again even though you're worried you might be dying. You're still bleeding. It's still heavy. He tells you once he finishes that he wishes he had known your period was coming because he wanted to go down on you. You smile at him, run your fingers down his cheek, and feel immensely sad that you might die before that happens.

As he thrusts into you on the third day of your bleeding, after you've gotten back from your work shift, you consider going to the hospital once he finishes. He kisses you deeply. You wonder if he can taste the blood from the lip you chewed through. You think maybe it's time to get help for the other place you're bleeding from, to figure out if this is normal, if there's something wrong with you, if you're dying and should get your affairs in order.

You still enjoy yourself, still enjoy the feeling of his body against yours and you wish you could stay like this forever, wish that it would never end. You think that if this kills you, at least it was a good time.

He finishes.

You go to the bathroom, sit on the toilet and google the address for the local hospital. You stare at the photo of the hospital until your screen turns off.

You don't go. Somehow dying sounds better than admitting to a stranger in a white coat that you went to Catholic school, that you never got Sex Ed, that you were a virgin three days ago and now you're not and you haven't been able to stop bleeding since and you're worried that maybe you were wrong in all your atheism and maybe God does exist and he's punishing you, trying to kill you now for being a fucking redskin slut and once you've bled to death, he'll send you to hell for the things you've been doing with that white man lying in bed, waiting for you to return.

You close the Google search tab. Flush the toilet and wash your hands. You stare at yourself in the mirror until you've wiped off the panic from your expression. You even get your fake smile to touch your eyes. You leave the bathroom and join him again. He holds you close, kisses you. You almost tell him. But you don't. Just like you won't tell him two months from now that your period hasn't come and you were several hours late taking a pill the month prior. You won't tell him because you were taught to keep things like that to yourself, to deal with it alone, and you're also worried he'd be mad at you and blame you for being careless and you can't stand the thought of him hating you like you hate yourself. And you won't tell him when your period finally does come because what's the point of scaring him with that now, just add it to the list of things you don't tell him because you were never taught proper communication and it's not like you can sign up for a class and learn it now. And you'll never tell him you love him, even though you do, because you don't think he could love someone like you, you don't think someone like you can be loved, redskin sluts like you are unlovable. Maybe you're right because he'll leave you before you ever have the chance to say the words.

You stop bleeding on the fourth day.

THE FALSE PROPHET OF
NEW BEGINNINGS
MARK BESSEN

I woke up in my dorm room, my face buzzing and my tailbone aching, with firefighters leaning over me, only they weren't firefighters, they were strippers. My friends, now standing along the walls of the room in reverence of the scene, their faces absurdly solemn for such an occasion, those prudes, had ordered the strippers to celebrate something I couldn't recall but felt excited about nonetheless, so I asked them (the firefighter strippers, not my friends) to please start the show over, I must have missed the beginning.

"Do you know where you are?" one asked as I reached for his bulging bicep.

I was impressed with his character acting, the way he set the scene. I told him of course I did, this was my dorm room, but I wouldn't mind moving this to his place if they all preferred.

The words were falling out of me, like I wasn't speaking them so much as they were pouring forth from a natural spring that bubbled language up from the depths of me. I could watch the words emerge, watch the letters form and drop from my mouth, could even alter their shape, their font, so I confirmed that what I was telling them had come out in a clean and respectable Garamond.

"Do you know what day it is?"

I could tell from the way the chill air plucked at my vocal cords and the cacophony of birds outside that it was a Tuesday, so I said so, and that seemed to ease their imagined concerns a bit so they could get on with things.

I heard them ask one of my friends if we had any drugs, which seemed a bit presumptuous since we'd been the ones who hired them, and she shook her head.

I realized I still had a hold of the firefighter's bicep but hadn't clarified the touching policy, so I let go and laid back onto the floor.

My new job as an analyst at a Big Bank came with a corporate credit card with a ten thousand dollar spending limit, to buy the accessories required of an analyst and help with the move. But I wasn't moving, and all I needed was a computer, so I bought that and spent the remainder on presents for everyone who helped form me into the rhombohedral shape I was.

The interview had been a blur—nerves, naturally—and I found that, while I had no memory of the face of the interviewer or the content of the interview, I was so enamored with the texture of her dress—something between a microscopic waffling and a disintegrating tweed, a bird's nest shrunken and flattened—that I was thrilled to start work, analyzing whatever needed analyzing.

I asked the person I'd met at the career fair (a recruiter, perhaps, but who really knows with these big companies) for the number of an HR rep, because I'd lost the interviewer's contact info, but the HR rep was perplexed when I asked about reimbursement for the ten thousand dollars. Surely she was new, and it would show up in my first paycheck. I would start the week after graduation, just a few months away, not long enough for the accrued interest to be too daunting.

The ends of things have always been hard for me, mostly because ends are really beginnings, and beginnings have always been hard for me. The spring semester of my senior year in high school, just months from graduating, I got so depressed I became catatonic, and, after a rather-too-aggressive medication regimen fastidiously implemented by my mother (who, I will say, received the best of the presents I bought—a white-gold sea turtle necklace with a mother-of-pearl shell), I began to hallucinate. I wasn't seeing things that weren't there, but the things that were there wouldn't stop moving,

oddly and disconcertingly. Faces, especially. Any face I saw accor-
dioned up and down, stretching and contracting like its bones had
been replaced by slinkies. Noses were the worst, confirmed by my
mother's foot-long horse's snout as she administered my morning
medication.

So, rather than see faces, which would never look quite right
again, not ever, I closed my eyes and slept. I'd made it through the
fall semester with perfect grades and sent off my college applications,
receiving multiple acceptances from Fancy Schools that I had ranked
according to distance from home (farthest first). So then, in spring,
I just had to not fail out, which proved impossible without opening
my eyes. My teachers, ready to be done too, were accommodating,
and sent all of my school work home. I ordered solutions manuals
online, and, mustering the energy it took to fill in my pages of work,
I successfully graduated, though I never attended the ceremony and
was not one of the twenty-two valedictorians (a distinction granted
by the school to help pad its graduates' resumes).

Which brought me here, to the end of another senior year,
but college this time. It had taken six years, working on a reduced
course load during the six to nine months a year I was debilitat-
ingly depressed, and chugging through economics textbooks when
my mind was cooperative. Here, then, not at my top-choice Fancy
School but at the one with the most amenable mental health policies
to palliate my mother's concerns, I had just a few months left before
I would reach the Goal, the cushy corporate job at the end of a
long and grueling twenty years of educational hoop-jumping that
promised to bring me Satisfaction and Joy and Fulfillment.

When the strippers left, I worried I'd done something to offend them,
so I checked with my friend, the one who they'd asked about drugs.

"Those were firefighters," she said.

"I know," I said, angling my face towards her as I wink-wink-ed to
let her know I was in on it.

"Like, paramedics."

"Whatever they call themselves, they were hot. Were they students?"

My brain had developed an exoskeleton (not my skull—inside my skull), such that even when the strippers took my vitals (a rather overwrought attempt at verisimilitude), even when I saw the ambulance's lights flashing outside through the window, none of this could permeate. I was invincible. All-knowing. Anything I needed, anything I needed to know, was safely inside the exoskeleton, which would protect it from the barrage of stimuli outside. And a barrage it was. I heard the lyrics of every song playing within a mile radius at once. Well, not heard so much as saw, like overlapping subtitles, or, more accurately, one of those pieces of art printed on a dictionary page, the words both part of and behind the work's meaning. The smell of Dino nuggets in the microwave down the hall and of taco night in the dining hall across the street tried to compete for my attention, but no need, I hadn't eaten in days. I hadn't slept, either, since … what, Friday? And even then, I knew I didn't really need sleep, so I turned on two audiobooks at once and began to synthesize Foucault in my subconscious.

I felt better than I ever had in my life. The novel I had started the week before was flowing like I was transcribing it from the Muses, none of the self-indulgent writer's block my English major friends complained about. I felt none of the lethargy that had weighted me down, none of the inaction, nothing: I needed to move.

I was pulling on my running shoes and heading out the door when I saw my friend, now holding my phone, turn the screen toward me to illuminate my mother's face, and though the volume was turned down I had learned to read lips, and she was saying Stop him, but I was not stopping, because why would I?

I made it six miles, each breath of brisk air like a hit. I ran through fields of lance-leaf coreopsis and snapdragons and evening primroses, of yarrow and Shasta daisies, names I'd never known before but that came to me through intuition as though they'd been plucked from the sky. I made it to the top of the dam that had created the university's lake, I saw a hundred years of sediment below the wind-broken waves, the chemical processes churning at the surface of the water, the generations of fish that culminated in the minnow darting through the shallows as I ran, ran, to the center of the dam, the lake level to my right, a cascade of concrete steps leading to the water below on my left. I ran.

But why run when I could fly?

They say I was out for three weeks. I woke up staring at a uniform. Only now the uniform was a nurse's scrubs instead of a too-tight EMT button-down, and I felt the tug of soft restraints at my wrists. They'd called it a suicide attempt despite my protestations that I had no interest in hurting myself—wasn't it unethical to hurt a veritable genius? I remember euphoria. I remember thinking, Thank god, the faces aren't moving, we've made it.

I remember it all as though from a life I had observed, or maybe seen in a movie, or read in a book, but still they tell me what happened. That after six nights without sleep, rattling on to anyone who would listen, I had conked out mid-sentence, gone immediately limp. That even after my friend had slapped me in the face, lifted me off the bed and dropped me on the floor in an attempt to carry me to the campus wellness center, I would not wake up. That my friend then left me where I was and called 911, but that, with stable vitals and no artificial substances beyond the prescribed in my system, there was little that could be done before I ran off.

I really did have the job, the interviewer having mistaken my mania for enthusiasm, though nothing but a tragically misinterpreted credit card ad could explain the ten thousand dollars.

A runner near the dam had seen me go off the edge like a ship over the horizon.

I remember the fall.

The flight.

The end, the beginning.

Right to Life
Dion O'Reilly

"I wish I'd been born a bird instead," he said. "I wish we'd all been born birds instead."

—Kurt Vonnegut

My mother hated her smell,
her body hair—
depilatory, antiperspirant,
FDS ozoned between her legs,
a soap-soaked flannel
scraped through *dirty bits*.
The house was full
of dog must and cat scat,
but she dressed
in pressed collars,
her bunioned toes
stuffed into stilettos,
her tits lifted in bras
named for self-propelled,
underwater missiles.
And my father—how she loved
to beat a weak man,
but be entered
by him as he cried

for forgiveness.
And so, I was carried,
made manifest and raised
because it must be done
like painting a kitchen yellow
or killing dandelions.
She might have been
a sea captain, a magnate,
a second Stalin.
I wasn't her choice.
It's not that I wish
I was never born,
but rather that I'd passed
into the universe
some different way:
wind, dust, a thrush's song.

Prologue to "The Wildings," A Novel in Progress

Ayn Gailey

You like thinking about the vault. You often picture it, built into the side of an icy mountain on an island floating far above the arctic circle, shrouded in absolute silence. You find the thought of it calming, even though its nickname is The Doomsday Vault. Scientists claim its contents will make it possible to restart humankind after a global crisis of apocalyptic proportions, yet the vault does not contain weapons, intelligence data, cultural artifacts, or medicines. Nor does it contain the items you personally would want to help you survive an apocalypse: your favorite pair of sweatpants, your record collection, your Chinese grandmother's recipes.

The vault contains seeds. To be precise, 1.1 million varieties of seeds for plant crops whose fiber can be consumed. In essence, it's a modern day Noah's Ark for agricultural diversity, a plan to ensure that those who survive will be able to feed themselves.

You are drawn to this idea of a backup plan of these proportions. It means that no matter how badly we humans mess things up—and, boy, do we show a propensity for that—we can start over.

The last time you started over, it was 1990. You were twenty, and you left L.A. to follow a boy to New York City. Not the cleaned-up city you'll come to know more than a decade later. In 1990, there were 2,245 murders in The City and 93,377 robberies; 93,379 if you include the two unreported incidents of your car stereo being stolen out of your Hyundai hatchback in broad daylight. It was also the year the Central Park Five—a group of black and Latino teens—went on trial for the assault of the Central Park Jogger, creating a raw under-current of racial and class friction you could feel everywhere you went. If only the city knew what they would know ten years later: the Central Park Five, some of whom served thirteen years in prison, did not commit the crime.

But you put up with all of that. Because you were in love. Not just with the boy, but with food. Afterall, you wanted to be a food writer. And, New York City was THE mecca of food. Later, you'd laugh at the irony. L.A. was a city that fit you much better. You didn't need a wind-resistant umbrella or mittens or long johns. You didn't even need a coat because there was only one season in L.A.—summer. You could buy any fruit or vegetable you desired at any time of year, and you appreciated being able to find wonton wrappers at every grocery store, something you never found in Sag Harbor. You could drive a car anywhere you wanted, and you weren't in constant fear of being mugged.

How could you know that mere months after you left L.A., it would begin its meteoric rise in the restaurant ranks and rival New York City? Three months after you left, a young Austrian chef by the name of Wolfgang Puck would earn a James Beard award at his restaurant, Spago. His former pastry chef, Nancy Silverton, became executive chef at the Jonathan Gold-praised Campanile and intro-duced Angelenos to artisan bread from a tiny storefront known as La Brea Bakery. There was also Nobu Matsuhisa who would open the most celebrated Japanese restaurant in the world, making sushi a household dish, all from less than a mile from where you had once lived.

New York City lured food lovers from all over the world and you were not immune. The first time you discovered Dean & DeLuca was how you imagined other people might discover God. As they walked into a church or synagogue for the first time, breathing in the scent of wooden pews, or took in the light pouring through stained-glass windows of a centuries-old mosque or felt the profound silence in an ancient temple. That was like you being lured into the minimalist designed market, breathing in lemon-roasted rotisserie chicken, fresh bundles of herbs wrapped in unbleached parchment paper, aged cheeses from France, and the oak barrel of tomatoes prepared a way you'd never seen before in Los Angeles: dry roasted by the sun, and marinated in virgin olive oil, garlic, and basil.

On Fridays you took the A train to the C train to the E, then walked two blocks to meet the boy for lunch. You held hands and waited in line for what you had an inkling was the best falafel you'd ever taste in your life, from a little cart with no name, in the shadows of the twin towers (yes, those twin towers), from a man named Nabih who spoke no English. Even when you travel abroad years later, in every city you search for a falafel that might rival that one, from that stand and that cook whose whereabouts became unknown. When you do find one that looks hopeful, you never eat it on the spot. You bring it back to wherever you are staying. You put it down on the counter. You cut up green onions and parsley and sprinkle them on, then douse a little hot sauce on the contents of the pita, exactly like Nabih did. Even though it never happens, you hold out hope that one day you'll taste something close to it again.

In 1990, there were also fewer choices. In grocery stores, there were not the forty-two kinds of pasta available to the future you. Gluten-free was not a thing yet. Barilla did not make white fiber pasta. DIY meal kits were not delivered to one's doorstep. It was a pre-Amazon Pantry, pre-Tinder, pre-Google world. When you wanted food, you had to grow it or go to a market and buy it. When you wanted to know something, you had to call someone (on an actual landline), read the Encyclopedia, hunker down in the library or figure it out yourself. And when you wanted to go out with someone, you actually had to ask them out.

There were also seemingly fewer choices when it came to sexual orientation. LGBTQIA was merely LGB back then. Friends were straight, gay, bi, or maybe a drag queen. The term nonbinary hadn't been used yet despite a majority of indigenous cultures around the globe historically accepting three or more genders. Almost all gay leaders of rock bands, gay actors and gay politicians stayed closeted.

You remind yourself of all these facts as you face the revelation that the end of your relationship may be near. You ask yourself how you've arrived at this apocalyptic point, with no back-up plan, no personal Doomsday vault, sitting on a bench in the middle of Central Park, wearing a wedding dress—not a poofy white lace one, but a traditional red silk and gold embroidered qipao—contemplating whether to abandon the love of your life at the altar. Not because you don't still love him, but because you've seen the way he looks at the boy who loves him, too. You wonder why you weren't better prepared for this moment. Is it because you were distracted by your love for food? Your love for the boy? Did you tolerate The City because of that love? Because it helps to have context when life, as you know it, changes. When the city changes. When the person you love changes. When you, too, change, all because there are so many—and so few—choices.

To the Man on the Greyhound to Montréal

Naihobe González

The plan was to enjoy the Greyhound ride from New York City to Montréal, to alternate between my book (a used copy of *Sentimental Education* by Gustave Flaubert that I picked up at the foreign language section of the Strand) and the verdant landscape of the Hudson Valley and shores of Lake Champlain, as if I, too, were a character in a romantic novel. I didn't have enough money to take a plane or enough foresight to take the train, but I was on that tired metal bus, reading the book in the original French and embarking on a solo trip to a new city because, at twenty-seven, that was the woman I wanted to be. Worldly. Independent. A little bit spontaneous. And then he came and stood over me.

"Is that seat taken?"

It was—by my bookbag and my desire for space and silence— but the girl I'd been raised to be couldn't give the reply I wish I'd given: "I'd rather sit alone. Do you mind taking one of the many other empty seats around?" So instead I shook my head and placed the heavy bookbag on my lap, shifting my body towards the window. I opened the book, inhaling its musty scent. The typeface was small and dark, in the way of old books. Sentences had been underlined in pencil by the reader before me. The first underlined sentence was: "Frédéric thought that the happiness he deserved due to his brilliance was overdue." *So our protagonist is an entitled young man*, I thought. In the opening scene, he falls in love with Madame Arnoux when he sees her sitting alone on the deck of a boat. He takes a seat on the same side as her and observes her closely, feeling a "painful curiosity that knew no bounds." I underlined that sentence.

"What're you reading?" He asked.

I replied, polite as ever, though he could clearly see the bright yellow cover and the title in red caps. L'ÉDUCATION SENTIMENTALE. But he wanted to know more. So much more. Why was I reading that? What did I study? Where? How long had I lived there? What was my name? Where was I from? Where was I *really* from? I fielded each of his questions and follow-ups, my answers increasingly monosyllabic. Our "conversation" felt like a one-sided volley I tried to dodge. Balls kept coming at me, one after the other. I couldn't tell whether minutes or hours had passed, but time dragged, exhausting me. During a brief pause, I grabbed my headphones out of my bookbag and—without even playing any music—put them in. *There, now he'll get the hint.* I turned back to the novel, holding it up with both hands like a shield.

Frédéric also interrupts Madame Arnoux's solitude on that boat. Though unlike me, it turns out she's not alone: her husband, daughter, and nanny are also on board. Alas, they are no deterrent. After she and Frédéric exchange just a few words, he becomes obsessed with her: "The universe had suddenly expanded. She was the bright spot where all things converged." Were I not familiar with Flaubert, I might have initially misread his take on Frédéric. After all, even today, stalkerish male behavior is depicted as earnest and romantic. Recently, I read an article about a man who wrote one hundred love letters to a woman who'd given him a wrong number, leaving a letter at every house on the street she'd said she lived on. The story described him as "smitten" and "lovestruck." Online commenters wished him luck in finding her.

"So where you going?" he asked. "Are you meeting friends?"

I nodded, lying, headphones still in. Solo travel is a conscious choice I make. A small thing I can do to claim my independence, not from any one person, but from society, from my upbringing, from my fears. To sit alone on a bus or at a restaurant, enjoy a movie or concert by myself, to move through an unfamiliar place without the need to be accompanied, *as a woman*, even if it feels awkward or lonely or even scary at times. It's my own little act of rebellion, despite being, in virtually every way, a very good girl.

I wish I'd moved seats or at least said, "Sorry, I'd like to focus on my book." (I hate that I'm apologizing even in my hypothetically more assertive dialogue.) But I remained stuck in place, knowing my discomfort and annoyance would've been apparent to any reasonable person by now. Because he wasn't just an overly chatty guy—he was demanding attention from someone who very clearly didn't want to give it to him, and I began to worry. Would he be staying on through Montréal, subjecting me to this torture for the next seven hours? Would he ask me where I was staying? Would he try to follow me? It would be nighttime when the bus arrived, and more and more, he seemed like a man who would not take no for an answer.

I continued reading *Sentimental Education*, channeling my frustration with his frequent interruptions into Madame Arnoux. Despite her husband being at the root of her problems, she sticks by his side, ever the devoted, self-negating wife, while Frédéric continues to pine after her. Throughout the book, she remains at the whim of these two men—though back then, women like her had little choice. Her fate was more up to luck than up to her. Why had Frédéric chosen her on that boat? Why had he chosen me on that bus? Gauging by the many times strange men have told me to smile, I doubt I looked very friendly. Perhaps it wasn't about us as individual women. Perhaps it was about, generation after generation, men being raised to feel entitled. Being taught that they deserve our time, our attention, our nodding, smiling faces.

Growing up, I wished to be treated like a boy. Like many girls, I went through a phase where I hated skirts and the color pink. Even though it was just my mother and me, the male gaze was ever-present. There were extra rules and limitations and hand-wringing imposed on me as a girl, because I had something boys wanted, and according to some, even needed. Whether want or need, it was expected they would take it. Sometimes they even killed for it. As I grew older, from my teens into my twenties, my mother's intense worrying about me and my safety made me want to hole up in my bedroom some nights. I had already stayed home for college, for reasons having to do with finances as much as cultural expectations and my mother's fragile psyche. Why bother with the real world out there? Books were a safer way to travel.

"I can die in peace once you're married," my mother would say, worried I would have no one to take care of me after she was gone. Surely she felt legitimately anxious that, I, an only child of a single immigrant mother, had no other family on this entire continent to rely on. But it was more than that. Marriage—to a man—brought safety and legitimacy to a woman. I could see it in Flaubert's novels as much as in the telenovelas we watched. For Madame Arnoux, as for Madame Bovary, marriage was more than an expectation; it was a necessary protection. Yet it also held them back, as Flaubert (if not telenovela writers) showed. A hundred and fifty years later, I wonder how much that tradeoff between safety and freedom has shifted for women. I was lucky to find a man who hadn't been raised to take what was not given to him, and I married him at twenty-seven. I could sense my mother's relief when she walked me down the aisle and handed me over to him. People say marriage ties you down, but I felt a little freer.

I began traveling my freshman year of college. There was so much I loved right away about travel, but perhaps especially how empowering it felt to explore someplace unfamiliar. As soon as I got my green card, I started going abroad to countries that accepted my burgundy Venezuelan passport, buying cheap sale tickets on Spirit Airlines. The world opened up even more when I got my blue American passport and jobs that didn't pay by the hour. I took my first solo trip in graduate school (Spain at twenty-three), deciding that fear—whether mine or my mother's or anyone else's—was not reason enough to stay put. Or more precisely, I decided that I did not want to be the kind of woman who let fear keep her from enjoying the world.

Montréal was my first solo trip since my wedding. My gold-and-diamond band visibly proved my status as a married woman, though this time it was real. Every solo female traveler knows the advice: wear a ring, whether you're actually "taken" or not. The thesis is that men are more likely to respect an invisible man than the flesh-and-blood woman in front of them.

I flashed my wedding ring each time I turned the page, as if holding garlic in front of a vampire. But like Frédéric, he was undeterred.

"So how long you staying in Montréal?" He asked, turning toward me. I lowered the book and made my already small body even smaller, crossing my legs and arms. And I replied.

I bought *Sentimental Education* because I'd loved *Madame Bovary* in high school. I both disliked and related to Emma, judged her while rooting for her. At seventeen, how could I not feel for a young woman who wanted more from life but was constrained by society? "She wanted to die," Flaubert wrote in 1856, "but she also wanted to live in Paris." I would've made this my senior yearbook quote if that had been a thing then. But Emma was not who I wanted to be. I wanted to be Flaubert, brilliant writer and world traveler who never married or had children. Like him, I was opposed to having kids, believing it was best to "transmit to no one the aggravations and the disgrace of existence."

My mother moved alone, from Caracas to Paris, around the age of twenty-seven to pursue a doctorate degree, which I am sure is the seed for my own love of education, travel, and francophone culture. We are our mothers' daughters, after all. This was back in the early eighties, before I was born. There have been many times when I resented her overprotectiveness of me in light of her own independent past. But maybe her concerns stemmed from her personal experiences as much as outdated gender and cultural norms. She once told me that when she learned she was pregnant with me at thirty-five, she had wished for a son. "Why?" I asked, a little girl at the time. "Because women suffer too much in this world." I didn't tell her that I, too, wished I had been born a boy, if only so she wouldn't worry so much about me all the time. Now I also realize that if women suffer so much, it's largely because of men. But I suspect she has long known this.

I also didn't tell my mother I went to Montréal by myself. She would have asked why my husband hadn't come, told me to share the Greyhound and Airbnb confirmations with her, sent me an article with local crime statistics. It's one thing to learn how to manage one's fears; it's another to carry the weight of someone else's. Well into my thirties, I still find myself putting off telling her about my solo trips. But I am working on it. This also takes courage.

The bus slowed to a stop at Albany. It had been only a few minutes since he'd last spoken to me, still oblivious to my book, headphones, body language, or growing curtness. I bore my gaze onto the yellowed pages of the book, though my attention was fully on him. From the corner of my eye, I watched as he stood up and looked down at me. "It was great talking to you," he said. I gave a nod and turned away in a manner I hoped canceled out the nod, lest he interpret it as encouragement. It was important to be polite, but not too polite. When he finished gathering his things and waved goodbye, my back relaxed into the seat at last.

But he never fully went away.

He was there when I checked into my Airbnb that night and found the "private room" I'd booked was more of an alcove without a lock. He was there when the young men who lived in the house came home, drunk and loud. He was there when I climbed up to Mont Royal and the long, leafy path down looked deserted. He was there when it was just me and a strange man in the metro car. I did forget him at times, like the morning I spent browsing through the Marché Jean-Talon, or when I went to see a French comedy in the Quartier Latin. For four days, I practiced my rusty French and soaked in the summertime charm of that multicultural city. But even after I came home with memories of a new favorite place, he was still with me. Because he'd shown me I was not the woman I wanted to be. I was too passive, less willing to cause discomfort in others than to bear it myself. I had allowed him to make me feel helpless and afraid, and I carried a grudge against the both of us.

Shortly after the bus ride, I wrote him into a scene of my first novel. In that version of events, my protagonist—a young woman who loses herself to an abusive relationship in a foreign country— manages to shut him up. I wrote: "She could feel herself getting more irritated, at the man and at her ingrained politeness. 'I'm going to take a nap now, okay?' She said, turning her back to him and closing her eyes." By this point in the novel, my protagonist has lost much of her confidence, and some members of my writing group thought she wouldn't have been so assertive with the man on the bus. Maybe they were right—maybe I'd wanted a re-do in my fiction. I listened as the discussion moved beyond what I'd written. Every single woman in the group had a similar story of crossed personal boundaries by a man on a bus, train, or airplane. The men—all "good guys"—were surprised; no one had ever bothered them quite like that, and they certainly had never done anything like it themselves. But if not them, then their friends or friends of friends had had to have done it. I wondered: why had they never noticed?

Months later, after he left the group, one of the women told me that one of the men had put his hand on her leg when he drove her home. She never accepted another ride from him, but she continued to read and comment on his writing twice a month "for the sake of the group."

When I think of my trip to Montréal, I remember not just the poutine at La Banquise or the smoked meat at Schwartz's Deli, I also remember the hours I spent stuck on that Greyhound inches from his hot breath, begrudgingly listening and responding to question after question, angry yet afraid of upsetting him, second-guessing my own discomfort. In motion yet stuck. Because even now, as I write this, I worry: will readers think he was just a socially awkward guy and that I overreacted—am still overreacting? And at the same time, I am ashamed to be the woman who didn't react *more*. The anger and self-doubt compound when I consider all the time I've spent thinking about him, when I am surely but a speck in his story, one in which he is a nice guy, a good guy, a classic protagonist and hero.

The standard novel plot is often described as a series of failed attempts that eventually lead to character growth. Neither *Sentimental Education* nor *Madame Bovary* fit this mold: each ends tragically. Emma famously poisons herself, never having stepped foot in Paris. For her part, Madame Arnoux finally gives in to Frédéric's years-long infatuation at the very end of the novel: "When they came back to the house, Madame Arnoux took off her bonnet. The lamp, placed on a bracket, threw its light on her white hair. Frédéric felt as if someone had given him a blow in the middle of the chest." Unlike his vision of her, the real woman standing in front of him had aged, something women still try their hardest not to do. Then again, his obsession was never truly about her. Once he had her, he lost all interest.

Every day, women's stories, real and imagined, end in tragedy. It's been years, but I still think about my failure to exert my will over him and the other too-insistent boys and men before him. He was not my first failed attempt, of course. And he likely won't be my last. It's no wonder we're raised to be afraid and that we fear for our daughters. But each time I travel solo—each time I take any kind of risk—I am telling the cautious little girl I was raised to be that fear, like gender, does not have to be a sentence. That it's okay to move through the world, take up space, make a scene, and to do it alone. She is starting to believe me.

flash fiction

SHE COULD DO WHAT SHE WANTED

JENNIFER BLACKMAN

The housewarming started like this: one of the wives, the one in overalls, fell butt-down onto the cool grass, the remains of morning dew seeping into her underwear. Damp undies didn't matter with the noon sun a reminder on the back of her neck—*You are alive! You live!*—and then everyone was sprawled on the cool grass and off their shoes went. A picnic!

"We needed this," a few people said. "We earned it," the others agreed.

A couple of hours into things—fingers fondling grass, beetles fondling grass, a dozen middle-aged bodies on thin blankets smashing grass—an old friend, really more of a lifelong acquaintance, asked the wife in overalls, her undies dry but not forgotten, how she "got into" birding, which is always how it's put: How did you *penetrate* birding?

"My cat," the wife said.

"You've always been so funny," the acquaintance said.

The wife was not here for this woman, no offense to this woman, and under normal circumstances she would not have put her health at risk for her, no offense, but in this moment she felt it suddenly, sharply—small talk, what a goddam privilege. "She's indoor. And watching her, like, moan at what she can't have outside..." She leaned back, indulging in the gentle ache in the flesh of her elbows, the chaotic grass impressions, and she closed her eyes. She let the sentence hang there. What would she say next? The wife was not there for this woman, but everyone was there for someone.

The wife's husband asked another husband if he thought social media posed an existential threat, and a faraway faction of the yard exploded with laughter, lit right up. Someone behind the barn called out "Jabroni!" Another familiar feeling, another sweetness—the desire to be part of a louder conversation, to be within every surprise.

A husband, this was the one whose housewarming it was, brought out a bottle of tequila and a bag of citrus, a paring knife, sea salt, a rocks glass for each couple at this picnic of ten, twelve, fourteen; whatever the number, it was below the health department's limit on outdoor social gatherings. A risk, but when you think about it, there's always a risk in other people. When you really sit down, undies damp in damp grass, and think about it. At least they were under the sun's UVAs, UVBs, UVCs, et cetera, cells, virus, protein coats all dying a swift death under magnificent, radiant radiation. And the breeze! Air tickling leaves and wispy temple hairs! This is what it means to be away from it all. This is what it means to be upstate.

They wanted to gather in groups, all these husbands and wives, and they did not want to hurt each other, but one must be ever vigilant these days.

"You got into birds for the moaning?" the housewarming husband said. The wife, our central wife—not his, she'd volunteered to show the latest arrivals around the acreage—had satisfied him by finding a way to bring up moaning. She had felt him pressing into the conversation from across the circle, which she liked, even if the whole afternoon she'd been giddier than she wanted, attention splintered, a by-product of social muscle memories rebooting. But the tequila had smoothed her pointier reactions—to avoid using the bathroom and compounding the risks of indoor contamination, she drank mostly tequila—and the sun would fall, too soon, and with it its protective UVAs and UVBs, and she was ready to play. She took this opportunity to look at him. The wife directed her attention toward the housewarming husband, making him, in this moment, the husband, our central husband. Life is about choices.

"I wanted to call whatever she was moaning at by name," the wife said. "Then I started noticing birds everywhere. It was like I'd never seen a robin before."

"Maybe you hadn't," the husband said. And she knew it was true. How to see what you're looking at? It takes practice, a practice of seeing. The pair locked eyes like they'd been dared, and she was fifteen again. How old did he become? Perhaps he stayed thirty-seven. She noted his inky lashes, spearmint-bright irises, possibly flecked, hard to say at this distance. She wasn't drunk enough to inspect his flecks with her binoculars, but she could, she could crawl to him, streak her knees with mud. Overalls made for unrestricted muddying. When she spotted a new bird, she described it aloud: olive wings, pale breast, fine sharp beak. Hear yourself speak. Don't look away, take him in. She could remember a bird in its compact and perfect entirety for only a few seconds.

A happy sleepiness pervaded. It wasn't the wife's job to talk, but there was nothing to see in the trees except the fading of the day. Most people enjoy a sunset, but the wife wanted something with a heartbeat. The tequila had uncoiled her, a body without nerves, a body that could hover and observe. She thought of a hummer before a puckered flower, heart rate eight hundred beats per second. What could the wife do in a second? She licked her lips and was rewarded with salt crystals. Should they order pizza?

"What did you tell me about birds mating for life?" the wife's real husband asked, his head appearing dependably over hers.

"Are you thinking about having kids?" the acquaintance asked the wife and not the wife's dependable husband. Ha!

"Songbirds do," said the husband whose housewarming, tequila, trees, salt, and sun it was.

"But they only have a fifty-fifty chance of living through the year," the wife said. "Bad odds."

After pizza, the wife's husband found his sneakers. "You have everything?" he asked her and unlocked the car with a beep. The parking brake was on, flat gravel be damned. She wondered how much of him was habit. The wife looped a surgical mask over her ears and said, "I have to use the bathroom," because she did have to use the bathroom. That's why she said she had to use the bathroom, because she had to. "I'll hold my breath."

The husband who owned the house and the house's cold tequila and the salt that burned the corners of her mouth, and the trees of birds and beetles, and the sun, and now the moon and the blue-black light of nightfall, this man was in the kitchen washing a paring knife. To his back was a screened-in porch cluttered with aviaries, ornate as cathedrals, not a songbird in sight. She entered through a side door, in the space between his back and the aviaries. She stopped to breathe and the breathing felt necessary and complete as it filled her up. She wandered into the screened-in porch.

"I collect them," he said. He set the knife down wet. He let the hot water run. He walked away from the rush of water and followed her onto the porch. He would lead her where she needed to go. It was easy to take a wrong turn in this new space, easier than you'd imagine, and she repeated this to herself when she took his hand, warm with dishwater. Spearmint eyes, rust flecked, blue outline, dew on morning grass.

They wanted to be together and they did not want to hurt anyone, but you have to be so vigilant these days, and some of us just aren't.

Migratory Animals
Lisbeth White

There is another dead deer along Hwy 19. Eyes glassed open and head at that awkward angle that makes a person roll their own neck.

I don't stop.

I can tell the deer has been dead for a while, probably hit sometime in the night, and I have learned it's better to just drive through tears. A few months ago, I did stop because the deer was still moving, still trying to get to its legs, which collapsed again and again beneath it, still struggling to cross over the highway now slicing its world into parts. I pulled over and crouched down, wanting to be near but not wanting to alarm it further. Its eyes were as deep brown and searching as my own in that moment, and I tried to hold the gaze with some kind of warmth and tenderness, something that might communicate, *I can't save you, but you're not alone. You're going and I'm here with you.* I decided to stay only as long as I could hold that kindness, and I made it probably five eternal minutes before pained grief took over.

I love a road trip, especially cross-country, especially on my own. I love watching a landscape shift from evergreen, to silvery bog, to high-crested alpine ridge in a matter of hours. I love not needing to explain to anyone why Lizzo's new album is the only right music to play while crossing the kind of desert that really is just flat hot sand, or why it needs to be played so loudly you can't hear your own voice even as your throat aches from scream-singing.

Being in transit calls forth an absolute presence with the self. As a human conditioned almost immediately upon birth to constantly attend to other people (was it my brownness or my girlness or both?), the moments of unreachability afforded by being "on the way to" are freedom. I'm time-traveling, zooming out of the grasp of the network, making a way somewhere, and YOU CAN'T CALL ME. Nothing to respond to but the road before, the horizon beyond. Nothing but going.

When I get home that day I tell Wayne about the deer and we look up who we can contact about putting deer crossing signs up along Hwy 19. There aren't any signs now, but hardly a day goes by I don't see a fluffy deer tail bounding into the brush after dashing across two lanes. Once, a tiny weasel took four small leaps out of the tall-daisyed grass toward midday traffic before darting back into the swaying meadow. *Good job, buddy,* I thought, *now's not a good time.*

But when is? We are all, all of us, migrating animals.

One quiet morning on the highway, my favorite acapella gospel music softening the air, a coyote trotted across the road. I slowed down, slow enough to see the wiriness of brown-gray fur, ears at an angled point. I can't say if its eyes looked directly into mine, but the eyes were direct, the look back to the road, purposeful. This look I've seen in undomesticated animals—so clear of neuroses and full of themselves, there's no room for anything else.

I had the urge to call someone then but have made it a practice to only drive when I'm driving. The one time I strayed was on the fifth leg of an eleven-day trip from New York to Oakland, hitting the desert between Arizona and California in late August. There was so much flat heat. The outside temperature read 115 degrees and there was hardly another being on the road. I called my sister, who, all the way back in Brooklyn, couldn't have done much to help me if my car were to melt into the highway, leaving me to die in the middle of the desert, killed by hot emptiness. But I just needed her to be there somehow, to be with me even as I was going away from her.

A week after the coyote sighting, a dead one lay on the other side of that same highway.

What do you think? Is it better for a dying animal to look into eyes mirroring its pain as it goes? Or should their last gaze be with the open road, on the horizon they were on their way to meet?

I don't talk to my dad much so I don't know who or what tried to kill him on his journey from the Jim Crow South to the Pacific Northwest, but I know every single one of my high school boyfriends got pulled over by the Portland Police for some reason or another. So when Wayne pulls up the contact to the Sheriff's department for animal and traffic related incidents, I bypass it and try the Department of Transportation instead.

The line rings for a long time before no one answers.

Woodhouse's Toad
Anaxyrus woodhousii
Nathan Manley

What mud-fastened soul strange as the stone's in you flinched,
   skittish, at the tamp of my foot? I, too, have moved
among giants speaking in the star-scented eaves
   of the world—poised at that untraversable league

past which the mind's lapse, landscape's heave, by blade and root,
   volleys through a heaven of thunderous discourse,
emptied of import, closing on a peace so deep
   the stultifying dark of it once birthed a god.

For I might have cherished, little toad, a stone's soul
   like yours. I, too, have loved as a stone loves that share
of life I take no part in: comb of the moraine
   and canyon's cut, the lung's articulation sure

beneath its structure. A field in Argentina
   sweetens December with strawberry air. The world,
as it's always been, is full. Not a thing shakes loose
   nor marshals up the grim, splenetic wit to drop

entirely out of it. Forgive me, little stone.
   I, too, have proved cartoonish—pressed like a daisy,
staling, dog-eared in some child's book. And for all that,
   I'd prove never small nor flat enough to love you.

There Is Smoke in Brooklyn
Shannon Huffman Polson

1.

A week before the fires, our youngest sits outside watching birds. He has oriented himself toward the mountains, the way the wind came, the way the water came, the way the fire would come. When he stands to come inside, he notices the trap—one more chipmunk, the jaws of the device around its neck. It has now been reduced to skeleton. I sit with him, working to notice every piece. The wasps have taken the flesh, the sinew, fur and organs. All that remains are minute wings of scapula and a fine white chain of spine and tail. What is unseen holds us together.

Early July. It is hot and dry. A lightning strike ignites the forest near Cedar Creek, ten miles down the ridgeline from our home. For fourteen days, the fire devours the heavy fuels in both directions, jumping containment lines and burning fast up rocky heights and through dense timber. Fire camps sprawl in open fields like military encampments, thousands of workers and acres of equipment in the valley below us. Fluorescent pink yield-shaped signs appear along roadways with alerts of fire activity. Fire information boards go up at major intersections and the grocery store. The aviation starts: helicopters, scooper planes, a constant overflight of water carriers working to slow down the flames, the sounds of a war zone. If it's not too smoky, they're flying all the fire lines. The sound of rotor blades becomes a constant.

I know the sounds of war, serving ten years in uniform, in Bosnia, Korea and places in between, and I know that extra attention that comes when what is around you wants to kill you. In uniform it was only me, a volunteer for the risks faced. Now we are four, my husband and two boys and me, unless you count the dog, the cat and two hives of bees (the kids would be appalled to leave them out). I've craved this haven all along, a safe place for a family, a place that extra attention can be turned to love and not to fear.

In the afternoon, two days after that examining the skeleton, a large white pickup truck drives up our road. We're two miles off the valley floor. Before the climb begins, a sign marks the road as "primitive." You have to want to come here, which is to say, no one just "stops by." It's the fire team division chief in charge of all fire operations. His name is Tom. Tom is nearly seventy, and wears a baseball cap, the dirty yellow canvas jacket of fire crew, and an enormous white mustache. He climbs out of the truck, I say hello, and my youngest and I walk with him outside. Peter joins us, and Jude climbs on his shoulders to look down at the map.

He spreads his map across the hood of his truck. He'd been fighting fires for fifty years and had been assigned to the fire from Oregon. For a moment, I didn't realize the reason he had come. The division chief doesn't just make social calls, not in the middle of a fire and not this far off the main road. The fire is burning our direction. We are directly in the path.

We walk Tom all around the house and I point out the work we'd done, preparing the land these past years—limbing and thinning the trees, burning all through one drizzly spring night. We'd pulled the bitterbrush. Thirty feet around the house we'd hardscaped with gravel and isolated low plantings, nothing that could catch and spread a flame. Peter's cut the grass back even further. I want the fire chief to see our family, to see we'd done our work, to see the thing I know he is assessing: this is a house he can, and will, defend.

I walk him up the hill to the well and cistern, assure him that we have water as he assures me they shouldn't need it. Our son Jude, eight years old, follows close behind, his skinny legs in canvas shorts hurrying to keep up. Tom stops to pick up a pinecone, his eyes crinkling as he smiles.

"This will open up and let out the seeds when fire comes," he says. "Do you know what that's called?"

Jude shakes his head.

"Serotinous," Tom says. "Can you remember that?"

"Serotinous," Jude repeats with a shy smile, looking up at the man who understood what was becoming scarier each day. Serotinous: when the heat opens the way to new life. Serotinous: another term for resurrection. Serotinous: a term that first implies destruction.

There is something comforting in knowing that trees here have figured out the way to survive fire. The ponderosa grow thick bark, and their seeds do best in ash and mineral soil. Douglas fir seeds like the mineral soil, too. Ponderosa is a masting species; they drop their lower branches, reducing probability of crown fires. But this applies only in the natural fire regime. The severity of fires threatens even these resilient species.

In my mind the Cedar Creek burn is still far away, something to watch up valley. We offer refuge to friends who live in the vicinity of Mazama and are closer to the flames. Smoke is everywhere, choking the valley in yellow brown. It's smoke you can smell and taste and feel, the sting of it in your eyes and mucous membranes. Peter and I walk the dog before bed, the smoke so thick we cannot see the stars.

Friday, I jump on Zoom to work on our new community library. When our call ends, I rush to pick up our eldest son Sam from river camp.

At the parking lot, my friend Suzanne walks over with urgency in her step.

"The kids are okay," she begins, though her words have to push through fear. "They may need to take a detour. But they're safe. The fire's not too close yet."

I'm confused. The fire is miles away.

"Another fire started off the Chewuch," she said. "It's running up Cub Creek."

Cub Creek is the area of the campsite where the kids have been for the past five days. My chest suddenly constricts.

At eleven, Sam had been asking for more time away, more independence, beginning that long work of turning toward the world that feels to a parent like a slow amputation for all that it is the natural way of things. We signed him up for a weeklong camp away at the river. The night before, my husband and I visited the camp for a parent evening. Our son sat in the circle confident and happy, his legs crossed just like his dad's, leaning into the conversation with bright eyes and a smile. The campers and camp leaders talked about the list they kept of all the flora and fauna they had seen, impossibly long—so much life!—how each camper had chosen a being to inhabit considering the effects of a changing world. There had been a lamprey eel, a frog, even a mosquito, and our son had chosen to be a beaver. His lean little boy's body was blissfully covered in dirt, washed off several times a day by swimming in the river and re-coated the moment he emerged.

For a moment I consider waiting for the bus in the parking lot. But what if the information is old? What if they are caught by the fire? What if they can't get out? I tell our friend I'll drive toward camp and ask her to text me if she sees them. She knows me well enough to only nod.

On the country road, I pray *Dear God Dear God let him be safe* and floor the gas pedal as the pyrocumulus comes into sight. The cloud burgeons toward the sky, a menacing mass only hinting at the conflagration beneath. I have no coherent thoughts. I've watched fire like this, I've watched it run and I've seen what was left behind, and what is left behind is sometimes nothing.

The cloud of smoke moves like a thing alive. Its form subsumes the landscape, becomes the landscape. It changes and grows with horrifying speed, claiming land and air, its size and momentum auguring the heat and flames, devouring anything in the path.

Cars have pulled over and people are standing on the sides of the road with cameras in a kind of horrified awe. They do not have a child at camp on the other side of that plume. I am not stopping for anything.

Suzanne's text comes just before I reach the road junction where the sheriff would have blocked the way. The kids are in the parking lot. She will let Sam know I'd been there and that I'd gone looking for him. I hope he will understand that I left to find him because I would give my life for his. Driving back toward this little boy, I am anxious to put my arms around his body, whole and breathing, and just eleven years old.

2.

We've made our home in the ecotone, on the border of dry forest and meadow on the side of a deep green ponderosa-studded hillside near the sage steppe and above a salmon creek.

As the snow fades, our neighbors return: the Say's phoebe and the white-headed woodpecker, the mountain bluebirds and the pine siskin, the evening grosbeak and the sparrows and swallows. All of us building homes to raise our young, creating a safe place where they will learn to fledge.

Now all our homes are in danger.

We had planned to leave for two weeks that Sunday to visit my mother-in-law, recently widowed, and send the kids to camps nearby. Get out on the coast and spend some time on the lake. This scheduled travel is now our escape.

The new fire, named Cub Creek for where it ignited, is burning north into wilderness, but the wind is pushing the Cedar Creek fire near Mazama through the dry forest and directly toward our home. Saturday, my husband and a friend don long pants and long sleeves in the heat to limb up trees around the house even higher than before. I take a trailer full of the highly flammable bitterbrush we've pulled from around our home to the dump. The fire division manager comes back for the second time in three days. The pyrocumulus billows across the valley, and one of my favorite bloggers reports that there is smoke as far east as Brooklyn. We are connected now, not only to every other living thing trying to breathe in the smoke, but to each other, across a continent.

We talk of fire as a hunger, a nearly sentient impulse consuming everything in its path. Seven years ago we moved our family out of the city, taking a risk for an adventure in the mountains. Only days after we first settled into our home on the side of the hill, we watched the lightning strike and trees torch across the valley. Small fires, we thought, watching with excitement and awe. They'll put them out. Isn't it amazing what lightning can do?

But then those fires galloped down the valley, tearing through grasslands, incinerating trees, uncontainable destruction. We watched then from the safety of our land, standing on a rickety porch, witnessing the ridgelines lit up for miles through the night, flares of flame as trees exploded, beautiful and terrible in equal measure. What would become the Carlton Complex was the largest in Washington state history. Until two years later, when the Okanagan Complex burned bigger. And five years later Cold Springs Canyon even bigger. Now it's our turn. Climate change and forest mismanagement is no longer an abstraction. The fire is here. It knocks at our front door. It may not spare our home. And from this fire, across the continent—there is smoke in Brooklyn.

Because of all of this, we built our home for fire. The siding on the house is cement made to look like wood. We chose a metal roof and tempered windows. Still, there are no guarantees. This ecotone, the place between habitats, is also another kind of border, the human and wildland interface. Our home sits on land surrounded on three sides by public lands, Forest Service and Washington State Department of Natural Resources. This interface carries with it a different kind of understanding. We do not want our home to burn, and we do not want to lose this land.

Washington state, fire evacuation levels:
  Level 1: get ready
  Level 2: get set, and
  Level 3: go.
All of us have "go bags" to grab as we run out the door, filled with what matters most for immediate survival. Evacuation levels can and do change on a dime, sometimes in the middle of the night. We drive away from our home perched on the hill above a gentle curve of valley just ahead of receiving notice of Level 3. I do not permit myself a glance back.

We are in Seattle at my husband's childhood home. West of the mountains, the skies are clear, while the newspaper from our hometown (and *The Washington Post*) report the worst air quality in the country. On the east side of the mountains, the same northwesterly winds directing the fire push the smoke into the Midwest and all the way to New York. Near to my mother-in-law's home, the lake is calm and smooth, the vastness of the water under blue sky a salve. To the northeast, we watch the pyrocumulous tower above the high mountains of the North Cascades, 30,000 feet and climbing. We check satellite images each hour, though they're only updated twice a day. Our home webcam shows the fire crews' activity. The National Guard has been called in to enforce safety. Friends text. Acquaintances text. Neighbors text. It is impossible to concentrate. I reschedule calls until the following week.

Tom, the fire division chief texts one night near midnight, addressing each of the four of us by name. I'm startled by his kindness in the midst of all that he must do. He gives a report of his crew's activities. They have nicknamed our house "The Fort," and are pleased with the precautions we've taken. They've laid hose and put in several dozer lines, heavy equipment cutting rough roads, scraping away any organic material down to the mineral soil, a line they can work to defend. They've installed 450-gallon water blivits outside the houses and set up sprinklers—what he calls a "water curtain." We fall asleep satisfied that we have done our work and the fire teams are very much on top of what else can and must be done.

The next day texts continue; my phone vibrates constantly. Gathered around my mother-in-law's table in the kitchen nook for pancakes, I sip my coffee compulsively. I sneak a look at the camera feed on my phone, holding it underneath the table while the boys argue over the last piece of bacon. Firefighters are now in full gear. One has an axe over his shoulder, and a backpack. They still move without urgency, but things have changed. A new truck is in the driveway. This one has deployed the hoses. It is hard to stay off a constant refresh of the fire map and the security camera, checking for new texts or emails.

But it is Sunday, and we are with the boys, and somehow I must keep that urgency away from them, protect them from my fear. Sam goes off to pick blackberries. Jude wants me to jump off the dock with him again and again: "Mama, want to hop in?" Boats crisscross the lake. Paddleboarders maneuver with leisurely strokes matching the languor of a summer weekend, hot sun, cool water. A few swimmers brave the chop, their orange buoys trailing behind them. The air is calm. The skies are clear.

At dinner, the volume of texts increases, closely trailing the increased intensity of the fire. It's flared again, the winds have changed. A friend sends photos. Another sends a video showing our ridgeline, panning all the way up the valley, furious with fire. Phones are not allowed at the table. My son who picked blackberries earlier in the day looks over and says with a look he learned from me: "Mom, can't whatever that is wait?"

I don't want to tell him why I'm breaking the rules. People are checking in, I say, and this is true.

The dusk at home is hastened by the smoke, and the angry yellow orange of fire blazes on the ridgeline where we've built our home, an unholy fury. Friends report trucks streaming off the ridge—the winds are tricky. The firefighters have been called off. Our camera goes down—they've cut the power. We were powerless before, and now we're blind. The longing for information is immense, and there is nothing to be had.

The boys must go to bed. They brush their teeth, and Peter reads to them. They say their prayers. We pray for the firefighters. I check emails and find pictures from another friend who lives across the valley showing greedy lines of fire ravaging the ridge for miles. I kiss them good night, and smile in the dark, hoping it will cover the fear in my voice.

"Sweet dreams," I whisper. And the one who wanted me to "just hop in" says, "Mama, did you get my reindeer harness?"

The other precious thing. I'd asked Suzanne to pick up the photograph he prized along with some art and pottery with the boys' handprints, but the harness Santa had left last Christmas, the one that was Dasher's training harness—how had I forgotten that?

"I'm sorry, sweetie, I forgot to ask," I say, "but it's going to be okay. The house is going to be okay and it will be there."

I kiss my boy who picked the blackberries and in the dark my silent tears fall on his blankets as I pray my words are true. And in the dark he does not notice, or does not say he does.

3.

We saw for ourselves the ongoing change made manifest when we moved into the wilderness of the West. Fire, once regular and cleansing for the forest, is now intense and all consuming. The combination of over-management of forest—policies known as fire exclusion pursued for decades and meant to minimize fire—and rapid climate change creates the perfect storm. The West is drying out, too. The drought map of Okanagan County stripes from moderate to extreme. That's nothing special for the West. Ninety percent of western states are under drought conditions, with severe or exceptional drought near fifty percent. Fires are burning in Oregon, in California, in British Columbia. It's hard to tell where smoke comes from. Each year we wait. Will fire come our way, or end up somewhere else? The only thing we know for sure is it will come.

The Methow people used fire for forest health when they lived on this land, before they were forced onto a reservation in 1883, their land appropriated. Fire, all Indigenous people knew, controlled the fuel, what we now call all that's growing in the paths of fires—the trees, the branches, thickets, pine needles, and any other natural material that burns. White people put the fires out.

Too late we realized how critical the fire is to forest health. Fire not only controls the fuel, cleans up the forest floor, but releases the nutrients from the organic matter—nitrogen, phosphorus, sulfur, and carbon. Most of the nitrogen is burned away in the fire, but these other ingredients enrich the soil. Too hot a fire depletes the land: where the fire burns hottest, the nitrogen-fixing bacteria can perish, further depleting the soil of nitrogen. Other organisms—endo- and ectomycorrhizae organisms which help to form relationships with and feed plant roots—can also be destroyed, taking decades to regenerate.

Now the government scrambles to burn and manage forests, make up for decades of lost time. They thin the forest where they can, logging efforts that may mitigate the fire. Washington State thinned on our ridge, but they've left the slash piles, bigger than houses. We'd hoped they would have done controlled burns years ago, but there is so much to do, so much land to cover, it hasn't happened. So much left undone.

To live in the wild place means submission to wildness itself, a willingness to live on its terms. Thinking we can fight the walls of fire is a kind of madness, worse still the lack of thought that leads to a belief in immunity from the hard necessity of what it takes to live—the brutal, clean requirements of cold and heat and fire. There are many people like this, believing that they subdue the earth by shooting anything they see or coming to the valley just to take, and to receive.

In truth, we were the latter once. It is the mindset of the conqueror, the peak bagger, the recreationalist. It is the mindset, perhaps, more of the young. I wonder if a different understanding has come not only with time living on this land, but also with middle-age, a shift of sensibilities as my youthful energy flags. The excitement I felt over a heli-yurt trip fifteen years ago is tempered now, blended with knowledge of danger and of risk, with a need for stillness equaling the need for action, with a fierce love for this family of ours and of this wild place where we have made our home. To fully live in wildness means to listen, watch, and learn. Sitting not to receive, but to know. To know and then to truly love and learn to give, to offer every day the prayer of full attention. Here is another kind of ecotone: that of safety and letting go. That of knowing and not knowing. That of praise and lament.

I think back to that drizzly spring evening two years ago, and on a school night too—we'd stayed up all night and done our own burns, lighting twenty-one small fires to burn the clearing we'd done the weeks before. Our home wasn't yet complete; we slept in sleeping bags on plywood floors amid the sawdust. The small fires were big enough to drive adrenaline as sparks danced upward into branches. We watched and calculated what was stronger—sparks or rain drops? Even a small brush pile throws off surprising heat, reminding you how quickly it could get away.

Life on these terms offers a particular intimacy, a deeper understanding of our connection to this created world, to the forest, the hills, the sage steppe in a way we feel in our flesh and to our bones. From the house, black bear and coyote run a corridor atop an underground stream. In ways we never considered in the city, we watch the grasses change color subtly over changing months and seasons, from green to pink to shimmering gold. We make friends with humming-birds. Our eight-year-old spots the goshawk in residence atop the snag, has learned to hear and see the red-tailed hawks and osprey, knows the wren's tilt of the tail and the flocking cedar waxwings. One morning, sitting outside with Jude, I saw a flash of yellow in the serviceberry.

"It's not a meadowlark," I said, perplexed, and he said, skipping inside, "Mama, it's a goldfinch." I doubted him and pulled out my Sibley's; he was right.

Any relationship involves compromise, and it is no different with the land. As the fires began their rampage down the ridge, one friend texted: "Hopefully J's hummingbirds scrammed!" And a local elderly man he befriended wrote: "Let's hope our big birds made it out." Another friend messaged: "It's not fair. You did all this work for your home, and it's not fair." Fair, I thought, doesn't factor into this at all. Fires burn where and when they will.

And submission—I suppose true submission, true release, would not allow for fear, but I am afraid. At night after tucking the boys into bed, the dark pressing against the windows, I pray for safety. I pray for our home, for this refuge. I pray for our trees. When once I thought the scale of what is wild dwarfed my concerns, I now under-stand they are not separate. The wild and we are of a piece.

We didn't hear what the fire had wrought until Monday afternoon. The day transpired without incident, a whole day without infor-mation except the phone videos of friends: ravenous walls of flame ravaging the dark, roaring in the wind over contours where our home should be; a photo of the red taillights of the convoy of fire vehicles called to safety and off the fire. A friend across the valley said he had to shut the blinds; they could not bear to watch the conflagration.

A text from Tom, the division chief, comes to my phone, addressing each of us by name. The fire burned through, but our home is safe, he tells us. I nearly weep at the kindness of his update—in all that he had to do, he sent us an update on our home.

The fire jumped the dozer lines, many times. It burned up to the sprinkler line. He attaches photos, a monotone yellow gray, taken from above the house. Everything is gray or black. Trees are gone or blackened. But our home—even the garden—still stands, unhurt.

Still, I can barely breathe.

My husband goes back with his camera for just a day to walk the burning land, to talk to firefighters and document the burn. The ground still smolders. Little spots of fire push through the ash after burning along roots below the ground. Firefighters walk around with shovels to put them out—mop up, it's called. The yellow jackets are furious at what's transpired. Everyone is getting stung.

The work limbing up trees paid off; many of the large ponderosa around the house look healthy, their thick bark evolved for fires and the lack of ladder fuels allowing the fire to burn through without harm. The meadow where light had played across the nuanced shifts of color now lies scorched and blackened; below the aspens, where thickets had held bird nests and the homes of other creatures, burned to white-gray ash. Impossibly, chipmunks still scurry across the burn.

"I'm so relieved," one friend writes, seeing the photograph of our home. "And next spring the lupine will be amazing in the ash they love so much."

There were still losses. The hundred-years old settlers' cabin in the aspen grove, the one I'd used as a writing cabin, burned. The new metal roof we'd added a few years ago is all that remains, twisted like rumpled fabric above the ash. Inside the cabin, I had set the rocking chair from my childhood bedroom. A beautiful old wood burning cook stove I used as a bookshelf. Now they're gone, this cherished marriage of past and future. At the end of the meadow, the old grand-father Douglas fir is gone, too. We loved it for the long low branches defining a secret place, tall enough for our whole family to stand inside, to look up into the ladder of branches reaching to the heavens. Because we loved those limbs, we did not trim them, and because we did not limb the tree, the fire claimed it, too.

Two more months of burning lie ahead. New Level 3 evacuations came last night. There is no room for relief that our house still stands; our hearts are heavy with the fear and uncertainty of our friends and other community members. The fire is burning toward the community of Pine Forest, where we know the trees grow dense. The fire season is scheduled to continue for many weeks. When others' homes are threatened, it is too soon for joy.

An email pops into my inbox from a local environmental group urging us to reconsider the damage of fire, consider it a natural cycle. I hit delete. It's far too soon.

4.

We return home four weeks after the fire, under an impossibly blue sky. Small spots of twisting smoke still appear across the landscape, trees still burning here and there. Each step outside of the thin envelope of our home compresses blackened soil and ash. With each footstep, a fine gray cloud of ash erupts. The crunch beneath our shoes is unfamiliar—the earth beneath has been reconstructed. The gentle slope of the hillside, once covered with sage and bitterbrush, is black. The curve of the meadow, charred black. Among the trees that stand, both dead and living, a young black bear cub wanders languidly and alone. We watch through binoculars. He paws at the black forest floor, moves on, and tries again.

Outside of a dozen or so trees near our house, the area we had thinned, limbed, and cleared, most of the ponderosa are gone—but standing still, trunks burned black and needles the color of weak tea. Below the aspens, the thicket of underbrush beloved by birds is gone, the land scorched white. Along the road, the place each morning and each night we walk the dog, the trees are gone—the trees that held the wrens and lazuli buntings in the spring. The serviceberry where the goldfinch hid is burned black.

It is not that the scene is an absence of life—it is that the life lost is overwhelming. It is as though the land has been bled. It is as though nothing can be safe. It looks like fear and I feel it like a fist inside my chest.

Our youngest son, the birdwatcher and chipmunk catcher, wants to walk through the burned areas. A few logs we had not yet bucked up lie charred, thick black marks on the blackened ground.

"Let's not cut down all these trees," he says of the pale ponderosas with the ink black trunks. "They tell a story."

But even for him, it is too soon to try to find the best in this. He worries about being stung and soon wants to head home, up one of the several dozer lines and not on the charred earth, as though death might be catching.

Beneath our feet, the ground crunches like leaves, like Styrofoam, like coins, and then suddenly, the soft pliancy of ash, an alarming lack of structure. Although the smoke has cleared, the air is pungent with the charred remains.

Where the bitterbrush grew thickest, the fire burned hot. Only the black twisted skeletons of these oily bushes remain, the standing dead, the charnel ground of land we love. Signs of life emerge from unlikely places: a tiny grouping of green leaves in the midst of the black, a flush of young grasses. If you don't look closely, you'd likely miss them.

Looking out across the char, the scars on the land still hold the terror of that night they pulled the firefighters off the hill. They hold the fear that no matter how we try to build the firm foundation of a life, that work can fail, too. They hold the fear of failing in this most important task, building a home and a family. They hold the fear and knowledge of erasure.

I stop and watch my son push ahead of me, up the dozer line. He walks slowly, thoughtfully, taking in so much for his eight years. At our feet, a few young green leaves push through the ash. Across the valley, clouds drape shadows over blue hills and a smear of gray-blue presages rain. Fire scars from years before cannot be seen from this far away. From a distance, it is beautiful.

The middle ground is hardest to see. The middle ground shows the devastation, the twisted metal, the sepia trees. In the gully below our home is the salmon creek. As a riparian area, it was protected from any kind of fire mitigation, and that protection means that fire climbing up the slopes feasted on uncut fuels, leaving whole stands of trees burned black. There are no needles left to soften the upright marks of the trunks. These patches of burn will not regenerate for more years, perhaps, than we have left. The definition of serotinous, after all, is seed dissemination delayed or released gradually, and gradual in the earth's time is long. There will be no quick extenuation.

Our neighbor calls it a mosaic landscape, but this kind of mosaic will take me a long time to appreciate.

To move to these mountains with my family means to invest myself and ourselves into the life of this place on the earth, to the earth itself. But in the earth's time, we are not even a fleeting shadow, not even a whisper, not even a breath. And still I believe—perhaps outside of time—we are a vital part of this world around us, that all of us created things are bound together in body and spirit in some way I do not and perhaps can never fully understand. Whatever strength or competence I've claimed is undone in this connection, the humility required of my place in the wild spot of ground. And for all that earthly time may disregard our passing through, for whatever mote of time I play, I want that time to give more than it takes and offer all my love.

And so it is more difficult to take in, in looking at those patches of black and sepia which weeks before were layered greens: the understanding of our sins, our own and those who came before; the way we've used our world for our pleasure without the deep respect that comes from love; the care that comes from that respect. The way we've closed the blinds and looked away. We'll have to tell our children the part that we have played. These failings are the reason for the marks we bear, our forest bears, our planet bears, the scars that will remind us every day.

We decide what scars will represent, what stories those downed trees will tell. That is the work, to see these forest scars as markers of resilience, a compass pointing the way ahead. For now, they still stand for fear. That part of grief must run its course. And then—the earth begins to heal and it will be time to make a choice in how we move ahead. Then those scars can take on new meaning and direction.

These little boys of ours will learn how desolation must be borne, and bearing it can bring that amazement that comes from loss and resignation leading to wonderment of life anew. And in that understanding, I can only hope they will forgive us, we who tread so carelessly on their inheritance. After all this fear, and what has been so changed, what will settle into the hearts of our blackberry-picker and our lake-jumper-bird-watcher boys?

The forest burned. The land is cleared. The chaff has burned away and we decide now how to hold the heat of what is lost in balance with learning new and deeper ways to love it. To love is to face loss in all its terrifying depths and keep on loving anyway, the land, each other. We are not safe. We cannot make our home invincible. I cannot spare my children pain.

One night, we sit outside and look across the meadow, a pattern of waves showing where the fire moved. The rain begins in tiny drops. The rain and the ground together smell of charcoal. I put my arms around my boys, their little growing bodies, and Peter puts his arms around me, and all of us are silent for a moment, holding all the shock and fear and pain together. I squeeze their shoulders and bend my head to rest against theirs, but they will not be still for long.

I smile and laugh and look at them and say, "Let's go inside."

Porous Rock

Demetrius Buckley

Stuck in some state pen,
jagged fence with two towers,

six phones to forty inmates, hard beds, heads
on iron pillows, some Studio 3

movie scene, Momma sanctified
in Cognac, pressing curls and spandex

slushed into an aromatic crotch. A new Iliad or idiot
when I thought I could be something worth wild.

Factory worker, father militant,
could smell a dirty taint like fried chicken.

He'd let bygones be bygones, shirt splotched
of another's—uniform, suit: some stick-up

kid far too young to recognize failure, faces and misfits,
Momma's mascara smeared, uncle's bowling shoes, his

prison release form framed, his heavy talk
of odor in older men, the crying of an older man,

the all too well of nothing ever getting better,
so you rock alongside, how Grandma

rocked you to sleep: that was just thunder—how
her hands were always oily, always

moving about to a gospel hymn. And I mean him
which is now a haloed sequence, a glare

through a prison window, a flash
on a sharpened shank, a tunnel with no end.

Dear Mr. Prisoner,

I only know you from TV screens barred by color,
heard your teary weep on a medium,

hands up for search to desensitize touch. Is it
that hard to do time? Thought you was bad,

street rowdy on intersection, minutes like
practice bullets and a sentence full of adverbs packing.

State shoes drag under uniform pressed by night.
Family severed by incision, phone

clunked on some yard with minutiae left
to explain that living is two steps parted in half thoughts.

Dear Prisoner, look how it got you, all beat with invisible
bruises that you grunt off a mat, exhale when they call

chow.

Twenty-four-hour sleep invaded, prison bars under eyelids.
Look how it got you.

Obsession

April Meredith Thompson

Between love and madness lies Obsession.
—Calvin Klein

The jungle carries waves of sound: sap dripping from a split papaya, the zap of beetle wings in flight. The roots of Banyan trees thread beneath the moss and crisscross like knees under a velvet skirt. When a line was drawn near the jungle to create a border, the trees shrank from their canopies, the roots recoiled. To make a territory you need a demarcation between this place and that. A line, not a wave.

Pushed to the brink of extinction, the tigers were brought back in record numbers—but they returned wilder and wilder. In the last thirteen years, the number of tigers in India has doubled and they have started to cross from jungle to farmland.

One day, a tiger swallowed electricity from a fence. Shock jumped down her throat. The black stripes on her back danced. She retreated to the jungle, the high saddle of her backbone loping.

To survive means, "to outlive, to continue to exist after the death of another." Originally, in the legal sense, it meant "inheritance." The tiger gave birth to a female cub. She snapped her baby's umbilical cord with fangs laced with lightning. The cub inherited the taste of shock, barbed wire, and a man-made line.

As the cub grew, so did her curiosity to cross that line and taste the sweetness of human blood. With her mother dead, she became the lone tiger prowling the jungle's edge. When she attacked her victims, thirteen in all, they lay at the border of farmland. Her classification changed from *endangered* to *dangerous*.

To bait her, they used a leg of lamb doused in *Obsession* by Calvin Klein. A bind of sandalwood, oakmoss, and most importantly, civet—her ancestors' prey. *Spray liberally on pulse points; neck and wrists.* These were the places the Tiger had punctured her victims.

Brown herons dot what's left of the jungle canopy and watch as the bait arrives. No wind in the jungle, just the rustle of green against brown, and yet the scent rides on the air, past lantana leaves and mango trees. It lands at the nose of the tiger and sends a signal down her throat and through her gut. Her pupils contract into tiny black beetles drowning in amber.

Little glass bottles filled with amber liquid sit in the bedrooms of women. Women who are mothers and sisters, daughters and lovers. At dawn, they dress for the day and spray their wrists and neck. They return at night to shed the scent of a cloying world. A world filled with the obsession of wild things, women and tigers. If to be wild is to be uncontrolled, then what is the word for those who hold their obsession against others?

In fragrance ads, the weighted eyelid is the symbol for sexual satisfaction. The trick is to suggest sexuality, without crossing the border into distaste. You can sell sex—but you can't *show* that you're selling sex.

An advertising man once wrote a guide called *How to Get People to Buy What You're Selling*. "Women need permission to indulge," he said. "It's basically choosing to unlock your own handcuffs. You're repressing yourself if you deny yourself this pleasure."

But those advertising men forgot that sex can lead to the worst thing for fragrance sales: pregnancy.

They caught that tiger who killed thirteen people. They shot her down. But her cubs still live in the jungle.

WRITTEN AS MALARIA HIT
DAVID MCDANNALD

South of Yokadouma, Cameroon, thunderheads slicked the trail. I gripped the rear rack of the motorcycle whose driver I'd hired for the trip. We puttered, waded, stalled, and crashed, lifted the Red Dragon over downed trees. After a night in the jungle and eight hours in motion, we reached the Baka village Ngato Ancien, where the storm had brought butterflies up from the clay, the surprise, not of petals sprouting with the rain, but wings. Children naked from the waist down emerged from leafy igloos with the motorcycle's growl. Men sweet with wild tobacco lounged under thatch, the old forest behind them not yet felled.

Baka here were said to live free of the Bantu legacy: fifty years forced labor for liquor, dominance in the bloodline. The elder, feverish, missing teeth, accepted my gifts of salt, soap, and jam and returned my greetings through a man who spoke French and Baka.

For those who lived separate and self-contained, I'd brought a question: "If a stranger came from a place no man could walk to in a year, a place whose people had lost their way, if a stranger sought the Baka for secrets in remaining recognizable to the past, what would the Baka say to him about how to live?"

A debate ensued, ten men clenching fists. They consulted the women, whose inclusion in matters elemental deserved credit for perpetuating a culture of four thousand years. A man with filed, pointed teeth laughed when I glanced at him, as if he knew such wisdom could not be shared.

The elder returned with word from the women. He sat, hugged his arms to his chest against his shivering, and said to start on the old path, I needed to dispose of half my words.

Or half my tongue.

"Or give thine ear to many and thy voice to few."

But nothing like this did he say.

The men huddled, asked me to repeat the question to ensure they understood. The elder came back with word from the women. Then he locked his gaze on mine and sighed. "To the stranger who came to the door," he said, miming a knock in the air, "I would ask him, 'Do you have any money?'"

I climbed back onto the motorcycle. My question, perhaps, was nonsensical; people who were not lost might not grasp how people could become so. Or else there was no place left far enough away.

HER RAIN IS MY RAIN
LISA BEECH HARTZ

I had three strokes, my mother says.
I know, I say. *That was years ago.*

I need more ways to talk
about the weather.

Sometimes
my mother thinks we live

in the same city.
Her rain is my rain.

This morning,
she heard the exhaustion in my voice.

What's the matter? she said.
You sound pale.

Dementia is not unlike
drunkenness.

People will tell you the truth
reveals itself.

For a long time
I wanted to believe that.

You're our best one,
my mother would say, blurry

from so much wine.
What she meant was:

You keep it pouring.
Anything to keep her

talking. Hoping for some revelation,
some residual affection.

All these years gone. Now, I save up
anecdotes to share. Small talk:

One son moved to Kenosha.
One son likes to draw. One

son wants to teach history.
One son got engaged.

I say their names again,
again.

Do you hear that? my mother says.
A siren wailing in her distance.

Storms coming. Better
stay inside.

Over and Over, but Only Much, Much Later

Michael Czyzniejewski

C arl, the kid next door, has made nearly a million straight free
throws. He's been shooting since he was six and hasn't missed
since he was nine. Carl's fifteen now and holds the world record, by
almost a million, nobody even close. He's been on every talk show
and podcast time and again, has been interviewed by every magazine
and newspaper, too. As he approaches a million, the attention is
reheating—the world can't wait to see him do it, so close, after all
those shots. In these times, he's become the feel-good story, the kind
of thing that keeps us going.

Carl doesn't know this, but I'm sleeping with his mother. Her
husband, Carl's dad, works downtown, just like my wife. They
carpool to the train station with two other guys on our street. Beth,
Carl's mom, thinks they're having an affair, too. This makes her feel
better about what we're doing. It makes me feel worse. The thought
of my wife sleeping with Carl's dad only adds to how fucked up this
is, doubling the dishonesty and deception. Beth and I do our thing.
We don't speak otherwise, save run-ins outside and the annual block
party. It's been that way for years. It works.

Carl shoots free throws in his driveway, at the hoop on his garage.
The free throw line, exactly fifteen feet from the backboard, has been
painted with the same red paint as the house—the line is ten times
brighter, the house in desperate need of another coat. Carl shoots a
couple of hours every day, two hundred shots on school days, three
hundred or more in the summer and on weekends. He's on track to

reach a million by the end of this week. Live feeds from all over the world will carry his millionth free throw—cameras have already been set up along the white picket fence that surrounds his yard. When asked what he'll do when he gets to a million, Carl, straight-faced, says he'd like to take up hockey, but will have to learn how to skate. America loves Carl. I love Carl.

Beth has one rule for when we're together: No talk about free throws. Her husband goes on and on about it every night and it makes her want to scream. When we're together, Carl is usually at school, but sometimes, he's outside, shooting his free throws. Carl always swishes his shots—always—but I can hear the ball hit the concrete, Carl dribbling back to the line, then silence until it repeats. Beth keeps me pretty focused on her—she has that talent—and we need to finish before Carl does, to avoid the obvious.

Aside from free throw shooting, Carl sucks at basketball. His stroke, while automatic, is too low to be effective in-game—he'd get stuffed every time. Carl is also no athlete, more what a kind person would call *thick*, with the deadly combination of stone hands and two left feet. His dad, even less athletic, never taught Carl anything—the hoop was already on the garage when they bought the house. I'm the one who got Carl started on free throws, me shooting around in my driveway after dinner—I even gave Carl his ball, the ball he's used for almost a million shots. Something about free throws stuck with Carl, and 999,000 shots later, here we are.

Beth and I always couple at her house. She says that's how we don't get caught. Her husband will never suspect anything, never notice the sheets out of place, smell the sex smell, or ask what she's been up to all day. My wife, however, would figure it out within a minute. I don't argue with Beth because she's right. It's also easier for me, never having to cover anything but my whereabouts. One time, my wife came home when I was with Beth. I heard a car pull up then my wife talking to the Uber driver in the driveway, telling him to wait, that she'd be right back; she'd forgotten some papers for a meeting. She'd actually called me a couple of hours beforehand to meet her at the train station, but my phone was at home and I was next door. I found this out when she got home that night. The beauty of it is that she told me what'd happened, but never asked where I was, had me explain myself, my phone on the kitchen counter, our car in the driveway, me nowhere to be seen. This is what makes all of this work, nobody suspecting anything. Or nobody caring.

The day before Carl crosses a million, he hits the rim on his 999,841st shot. I'm upstairs with his mother and I hear it, the distinct clang of leather on iron. I jolt up, Beth on top of me, nearly hoisting her to the floor. I peek out through the blinds and see Carl back at the line, shooting again. He swishes that shot, then the next ten. Beth asks me what I think I'm doing, standing naked at her window, watching her son play basketball. I explain what happened and she hesitates, but asks, "Do you think he missed?" I tell her no, that he'd probably be more upset, react somehow—no way he'd just keep shooting. "Oh, good," Beth says, but nonchalantly. I can tell she really doesn't care if Carl gets this or not, six years in, less than two hundred shots away. She wants me to get back into bed, but I don't. I throw on clothes, go out Beth's front door, into my front door. When I see Carl is finished for the day, I wander outside, and ask him how it's going. He says it's good. I tell him I heard the ball hit the rim and he nods, says he caught the front of the hoop, but it bounced up and in. He tells me it was the 999,841st shot that almost broke his streak. I nod and say cool, then ask how many he has to go. "Fifty," he says, and puts his ball in his garage and goes inside.

Beth likes to role play, more and more as time goes on. It started out with the basics, her a housewife and me some repairman or delivery-man, her in a ridiculous nightie as I pretend to fix this or that. For a while, we switched—I pretended to be the househusband and she tooled with the cable or dropped off an empty box. Things escalated, us becoming historical figures—Anthony and Cleopatra; Bonnie and Clyde; Charles Lindbergh and Amelia Earhart. We went through a celebrity phase—Richard Burton and Elizabeth Taylor; Burt Reynolds and Loni Anderson; Bennifer. Beth scripted world-ending scenarios: zombie apocalypses, virus wipeouts, worst-case Y2Ks, all adding urgency, though it didn't last. Lately, Beth has been playing a new game: anticipation. Instead of meeting five days a week, she cut it to four, then to three, and most recently, two. "This makes us want it more," she explained. I can't say she's wrong. But I also can't help but think I'm being played.

Carl has requested to be sequestered during his last fifty. The entire world, I'd guess, is watching online, on TV, on pay-per-view—Carl will not have to pay for college, or probably work in his entire life. The police rope off a two-block radius so Carl can shoot in peace. Units stand guard. I have a front-row seat from my house, ready to record with my iPhone, hoping someone will pay something for my particular perspective.

Just as Carl begins, I hear a knock on my front door. It's Beth. She's wearing a tracksuit but her hair and makeup look better-than-tracksuit, like she's put some time in. We'd agreed not to meet today, not during Carl's big finish.

"I want you to fuck me," Beth says from the threshold.

"Now?" I say.

"Right now."

Beth is here because her husband is home, watching their son through his window. My wife wanted to take off but couldn't, another meeting, but she's watching from her computer and has texted me several times. She keeps telling me to tell Carl good luck, which I of course haven't done.

I tell Beth that we should wait until Carl is done, that it'll take about a half an hour. I point out that a thousand reporters will come down on Carl after, giving us a window. I tell Beth it would be good if she were there for him, if she was standing behind him, her hand on his shoulder as he became the most famous person in the world, his fifteen minutes eminent.

"Plus, you should watch him."

"Why?"

"You just should."

Beth stands behind me, watching out my kitchen window as her son sinks shot after shot. After twenty-five, she snakes her hand down to my crotch. Ten more and she's unzipping my pants, pulling me toward the living room couch. I pull away, tell her that he's almost there. Beth spins me around, tries to kiss me, but I tell her no, turn to see another shot swish through the net. Carl is ten shots away.

"No?" Beth says.

"No."

Nine shots to go.

Beth tells me to fuck off, tells me not to come over anymore.

Eight to go.

"I mean it. We're through."

Seven.

"I think I might even tell your wife."

Six.

I hear Beth exit my front door. I don't hear the door shut.

Five.

Beth appears in her driveway, ten feet behind her son.

Four.

Beth says, "You can do it, Carl! I love you!"

Carl turns his head, then turns back.

Three.

Beth hovers right behind Carl, close enough to touch him. She looks over at the cameras. "Come on, baby! Do it for Mommy!"

Two.

"You're doing so great, baby."

Carl's next shot clanks the back of the rim, then front of the rim, then the backboard, then goes in. I almost throw up.

One.

Carl stands in position, glances at the rim, then at the cameras on the fence, then back at the rim. He wipes a bead of sweat off his forehead.

He's lost his rhythm.

"You can do it, Sweetie." Beth's hand is on Carl's right shoulder.

Carl lets loose the shot. The ball goes up and seems to hover at the apex of its arc, to stop midair. I can't bear to look and turn away, my phone catching the action, something I know I'll watch, over and over, but only much, much later.

ARRANGEMENT AND LAMENT WITH VOICELESS BILABIAL PLOSIVES

SEAN THOMAS DOUGHERTY

The rain falls
apart, percusses

against the roof
like a piano's keys

and pedals
plead the palimpsest

of present
tense with the im-

-perfect past
we used to sing.

What more could I ask
of the rain

than to explain
why your absence

awakened
me to stand in the door

of the night's psalm
unrecited?

nonfiction

Letters from One Disabled Body to Another Disabled Body

Allison Blevins and Joshua Davis

Josh,

I hear your *ache* from five states away—your fingers poised. I keep forgetting to tell you this sensation moves more like smoke. How it slips through curls, slips around my body—thick but weightless—into lungs to choke and curdle. I keep forgetting to tell you how I can't stop thinking about every person who has watched another person push a child into the world, so many lovers chained together, invisible filament: silver, pulsing.

Each morning, I push fingers hard into closed lids, electric orange-blue spidering. I float from my bed. A man sings my name in E minor, key of G. The sound of my name vibrates his throat and explains better my meaning.

Last time we spoke, I told you I'd become electric slivers like glass found under a cabinet months after a plate dropped and splintered. His singing is the sound, not of breaking or falling, but of my body trying to bind itself back to whole; the sound of the pieces of me in love and how they ache for the pieces of me abandoned on the ground.

My hair is falling out in clumps. You know the MS, but this feels new. I want to be literal now, but this is also every lover who braided and brushed falling too. Josh, write soon.

Dear Allison,

I meant to write sooner. If only I could string words between tin cans, like the cry owls hang in the night. I could find words to scorch your page.

Do you remember years ago, how after treatment failed, I sacrificed my hair so you would have a child? I wish I had a single word for my certainty, dull silver, gleaming like the small scissors in a hotel sewing kit, that each ringlet cut close to the root was a spiral in the spell. Such arrogance, such glee.

I need a one-word way to catch: "My father went to prison when I was nine. He was only gone a year, but his sentence was much longer." Do you have a thesaurus big enough?

When I watched someone push a child into the world, I felt an envy— colder, smoother than porcelain—then uselessness. How sharply could men adore if they could kneel and bask in the cindery glare of what they cannot do (though my husband did)?

Forests burn. My mother has been dead for four years, and I haven't spread her ashes. The singed trunks, kinless, will never return, whether or not I have known them.

Every time I write *I love you*, I hear *Do what I want when I want it*. No beauty promises an alternative.

Cross-stitched blossoms spread: wine stains, wide as a thumb. Dresses me in wounds. Dress me in slivers.

When we burn, we'll incandesce, I bet.

Josh,

I'm drunk again. *Miscarriage.* Is that what we should call it? I'm not sure how to even think. I keep imagining Sharon Olds and her drops like paint in the toilet. Something like that. You'd know her exact words. You always know. I laugh quietly, smile silently in crowds when it happens. Your quotations. You say, *That's it right?* As if you are unsure. As if any of us might know better. *Endearing.*

Pills too this time. I mean again. I mean remember how I spent my twenties trying to die. That want flashes still in tight gold strings from my hair like holiday tinsel. That old question, *What if?* Imagine. Imagine it. Here I am a directive. How the world would wake up again. How morning and dishes and sweeping and hanging rugs to dry.

This child would still be dead in my toilet.

A poet friend told me today—*I think I love you.* I feel the same. *I love you, too.* But here I am anyway. I want to cage grief in my hands with a swoop and clamp, trap grief glowing in a jar with grass and twigs. I want to wear grief like a dyed electric-blue wig. I want grief to rest gently on my shoulder as wings, ready for the melting. Where am I in the middle of this electric-skimming-cold, creped-skin-wearing grief? Josh, I want to say I am alone with it, but it is so dramatic. I can't manage the drama of *alone.*

I meant this poem as apology. For being in this room again.

Josh,

Now I am laundry, loose string snarls braid socks to jeans. Now I am dinner. Ham and box potatoes. I am inflamed buttons. Broken washer, water wrung from towels with my water-shaped hands, and the January crisp-dried terry cloth.

I've fallen again. Fallen to bathroom tile. Vertigo is normal, they say.

I forgot to tell you about the floor and the black that circles inside my eyes. I forget, always, to tell you how my son grows. I'll always remember the gleam of buffed tile the day I discovered I was pregnant with him. Your shorn head. How you were the first person I told. His feet are bigger than mine.

Someday my son will hurt a woman as men do. I want to remind you how you are implicated in this somehow—across the country, not his father, but a man all the same. What happened to the man who touched me at seven? Where is that man from college?

Now I am dishes. Now I am coffee grounds plunged and trapped against the bottom of a brittle glass beaker. Do you remember our trip to Oklahoma? What you told me in the car about love? Balance is affected by input, processing, and output. I can't tell where my feet or legs are moving. I imagine my past lovers are my father's old suit coats sold on consignment, hard gum and lint and a bag of my brother's confiscated pot in a pocket. Imagine them like donated hearts in the chests of strangers.

Dear Allison,

Today is Emily Dickinson's birthday, and although I will never downplay her joy—spiky, man-eating, untameable—I can't think of anything but her pain. Pain creased her knuckles as she kneaded the bread. Pain tinted the ink in the inkwell. Pain spread like chintz, and she stenciled the arabesques with a canny finger. Pain held her hand on the train to Boston and walked like a child behind the linens on the line.

Don't get me wrong. I know she loved, and slept, and sneezed, and got bored, but when I think of the Missouri winter inching across your blankets, I think only of her gashes, of her migraines, and of her: our bonebreaker.

Dear Allison,

I've been sleeping like someone inching toward a rage. No bedroom is dark enough. Moonlight hisses, immaculate, as if dropped into molten iron.

I could be a woman—if I were brave enough not to be beautiful. A mountain backs against a crackling blue daybreak like a teenager shoved into a brick wall.

Every morning I stoop. I shamble sideways to the bathroom. How does anyone bear the mirror? Every morning I remember Marge Piercy because she knows what I have to be—in order to button the cuff, to buckle the brace: *a warrior and a witch.*

What do I miss? Walking miles uncountable, limping, speedy, defiant. (The boys across the street name me *bitch, bitch, bitch.*)

If we were in a field—stalks dry yellow, fiery poppies bruising their own throats—I would scratch the scales from the gown of your old wedding dresses, and you would braid my hair.

Josh,

I told you I'm not writing. Yet you wait and wait and wait. Patient as a blank Mad Libs. Patient as yellow. Patient as your letters calling to me from Ohio, from Florida. Am I meant to save both of us? This sounds like an accusation, and I suppose it is. That is female work. Isn't it? I'm furious. You are not the cause. Yet. Here we are. I want violence—the blood of knuckles on a nose. I've only shot a gun once in my life. I can't do it again. But these long days I like to imagine punching someone. Imagine cheek and jawbone tough and tight under my knuckles. I like to imagine I'm the type of person who could do what needed to be done.

Allison,

Harder and harder these days not to begin with light—brick-broken, ground to powder, bracing, frigid, wet.

When I got your text message, I heard my heart, which had gone elsewhere. I won't say hammer, or pound, or thud or shudder. And I won't excuse either of us from that awful moment with an easy metaphor about a bird, or a bowl of cold fire, or anything carnivorous.

I know this: if it had happened to me, an alien sea would cover my head, shingle by shingle, and I could never escape.

Josh,

I can't discuss it anymore. Who types anymore anyway? I'm not the person I was. Not limp-walk, not drunk, mother who turns on the TV and walks away. Please let go of my words. I'm not here anyway. Imagine me the yellow glow of a bug zapper. Do you know this machine? Even in childhood, that death swarmed my hair. One hung, ominous, from the eave of our house. I remember the night I realized I would die. My first true panic. I've not let go of that beauty since. Like cocaine or cheating on a spelling test, anything I've done to feel alive.

Allison,

I almost became someone who, like Mary Oliver, would have been able to distinguish the scratch of katydids from the scratch of cicadas. See? There. There's the spot. Whenever my phrasing widens like a wing, I know I'm shielding a wound.

Yesterday, you were bedbound. I imagine minutes clustering around you or falling through you. I also imagine how wrong my visions must be. The lyricism's crass when beauty is a crutch. When beauty is a crutch.

But the unstrung harp is the one I want to play.

I used to think that living in my body was like spending the night in a ruined house.

I had no idea.

Why write another poem about the moon?
JULIA KOLCHINSKY DASBACH

Mercury has two days left
in retrograde and the Mars
  rover just landed on sands less red

than imagined and my son
  drags my daughter
around the house

  in an oversized box convinced
he is wielding an interplanetary
  time-machine and he slams

the box flap on top of her
  and means to do it
and time keeps going her lip

  split red the shade I expected
him to turn her mouth
  without intention and I've raised

my voice I've screamed violet
  too many times and turned
redder than I ever imagined

motherhood and when
nothing else worked his father snapped
        a leg off a Spiderman

action figure and threw it
        in the recycling bin and my son
wailed red and burning

        refusing to believe it couldn't be
fixed or time couldn't move
        back just this once or

my arms could refuse
        to hold him but we explained
calm and colorless

        some things once severed
can't be put back together
        some things like the moon

have to stay broken

Beige, Beige, Beige, Beige

Jesse Salvo

Julie has ordered a goat cheese and dried cranberry salad with a sort of Dijon dressing. She is the only person who ordered a salad. Mark is looking around nervously for the waiter to bring more water. In twenty minutes, unbeknownst to anyone at the table, the restaurant will begin substantively dissolving, the process beginning at the edges and slowly eating its way toward the centermost table perched on an inexplicable island of fake hardwood flooring. The boy, Bailey, is swinging his little legs wildly under the table. Occasionally his hyperextended knee connects with the table support and makes a hollow knock and one of his parents gives him a warning look as he rubs his leg smarting before resuming. Julie's sister Triana is scratching the fine blond hairs on her arm pretending to listen to Julie's story from work but really thinking about the waiter, his face, his carriage, the first time she ever slept with anybody (college), that boy's face, that boy's carriage. It's nineteen minutes till the restaurant edges begin to dissolve. Objects first smooth over, loosen, then lose their contours, color seeps out and they become a sallow fleshy beige. People walking by on the street will have one of two reactions: 1) cry out in horror, looking in at the foggy, writhing, tanned mass, or 2) avert eyes, keep walking, as when accosted by those bus station evangelists or sandwich-board fundraising types.

Mark has ordered the steak au poivre. Triana has ordered some vegan thing. Bailey likes lobster but his Mom ordered him chicken fingers because you do not order a child the most expensive thing on a given menu. Julie and Mark have just come back from one of the Carolinas (whenever Triana thinks she knows which one, she is corrected in the other direction) and you could confidently describe their faces and shoulders and chests as "freckled" or else "sun dappled" if you were being very middlebrow about it. The first person to notice the dissolution encroaching will be the line cook, who has been three years back of house here, suffers chronic knee and spinal issues from standing twelve hours a day at his post, and believes the CIA created and purposely spread the HIV virus in the US in the early 1980s. This conspiracy, of course, can be traced back to Cold War Kremlin propaganda, a rumor created and fanned by the USSR to damage the US government's credibility among its own citizens (namely the Black and gay communities which were being ravaged by AIDS at the time). Not that Uncle Sam needed any help casting doubt. President Ronald Reagan can be heard in several undoctored recordings, available online or via FOIA request, literally laughing at the idea that homosexuals and African Americans are falling ill and dying from Kaposi's sarcoma, pulmonary edema, acute immunode-ficiency, or sepsis. One can rather safely assume this arch and jovial cruelty extended beyond the walls of the Oval Office, into the larger US Security State, the larger bureaucracy of death, the fish rots from the head down, etc. etc., but of course this does not mean that the line cook is correct. The rumor was indeed USSR propaganda. Much like Triana about the Carolinas, the line cook is incorrect but in a forgivable direction.

Bailey is bored by the adults' conversation and fidgets ceaselessly. He wishes he had his truck, which is red. Little does he know, the adults themselves are also bored by their conversation. That Triana is thinking about a skinny boy who peeled off her skirts once in a college dormitory ten years ago. That Mark is zoned out, staring at the freckles newly appeared on his wife's sun-dappled shoulders. That even Julie herself is not particularly interested in the story she is telling (about a humorous misunderstanding with one of her coworkers), but feels some pressure to perform the telling of the story for her little sister, to maintain the gush of meaningless sound that accompanies an Adult Night Out, for there is nothing so dreadful as to sit together in silence waiting to be fed.

She often finds herself growing annoyed, or resentful, Julie, at the de facto presumption that it is incumbent on her, only ever her, to maintain single handed this fretful cacophony, this battery of callow verbosity, to appear always as this silly, chatty woman, all so that she will not sit in silence, her husband will not sit in silence, her son will not grow up in ponderous choking silence, so that her sister will find it interesting to be, and go, out with them as a family, so that they all will continue to make plans, continue to go out together, continue to muddle through, continue keeping their mouths and noses poked just barely above the pitch and yaw of a violent swallowing sea. Ten minutes. Her salad comes. Someone at the next table over orders salmon. It is Monday and there is that thing everyone says about never order fish on Mondays. Julie, in the middle of her story, feels an inexplicable resentment well up in her, feeling suddenly sure that, if she did not do the talking, nobody would. That her husband would spend the rest of their marriage zoned out, that his mind is a kind of camera obscura, a black box, a dark room where he develops images she will never be allowed to see. That she cannot for the life of her ascertain what excites him, what thrills, terrifies, even moves her husband, in any particular cardinal direction. Triana meanwhile, nodding attentively across the table, has the sudden urge to call her older sister a *cunt*, something she has never called anybody before. Understand, it is not that she thinks *My older sister Julie is being a cunt*, it is that the word simply pops unbidden into her head, almost decoupled from meaning, its rough geometric sound like an open palm slapping pavement, the image of her sister's and brother-in-law's faces recoiling in twin horror at the barking Germanic expletive, *cunt, cunt, cunt*, she bites down on her tongue to try and stifle this strange feeling balled up inside her stomach. Her skin prickles. Yesterday was her birthday.

Julie is one of those people who is very particular about when different parts of a meal should come out. She is the sort of person who is specific and pointed but still good humored when giving instructions. That a salad should come out before anything save the drinks, that a soup should be served when hot, that her son will eat pasta with butter. *Not* pasta with butter and salt, *not* pasta with butter and grated Parmigiano-Reggiano cheese, not whatever the chef in his infinite wisdom imagines her son will eat but what the child will actually allow on a fork to be put near his maw.

She tries once, just the once, at the beginning of the meal, to communicate everything clearly, cleanly, with precision, to a waiter who is preoccupied glancing down her younger sister's decolletage, and then does her best to put it away and think about it no longer, to smile and shrug if an order comes out wrong, to make light of light errors, to be always funny high-spirited wry flirtatious almost forty and staring past the mask of the face of the father of her child leering at her shoulder.

The line cook, stripping off a pair of acrylic gloves contaminated by raw shellfish, will look up and his face will kind of slacken, looking into … what exactly? Well not a void. Not in the technical, Newtonian sense of the word. A beige cloud. No, cloud is not even the right term, but the language lacks for a better one. Watching with loose uncomprehending horror as the dissolution passes over jars of canned preserves, microwaved fingerlings, a tub of crème fraiche that rotates seemingly suspended in midair before it is enveloped. Fructose, brine and aquafaba, all freed of their containers, seep onto the polished majolica pooling before themselves succumbing to dissolution, mere moments later, beige, beige, beige. The fuse box will be eaten next, dissolved, swallowed and the power will go out and a couple people in the main dining room will give little affrighted yips, nonplussed sighs, there will be some almost giddy childlike laughter at the sudden dark, a last rueful exhalation that precedes one of the waiters in back, finally laying eyes on the tan swirl and, watching it eat through everything in its path, come flying out of the saloon-style kitchen doors beside the unisex bathroom and eat shit on the rubber half-stair in the dark. People will rush to his aid and caution him against standing up as he tries splutteringly to explain that the entire restaurant is dissolving at the edges. People will laugh nervously the way you do when confronted by someone who is obviously mentally ill, the same kind of laugh you give when somebody makes an impolitic remark at a party where everyone is trying to make small talk. The waiter will open his mouth to speak.

They spent five days in one of the Carolinas just the two of them, she asked her mom to watch Bailey, Julie dropped the equivalent of two paychecks on absurd, baroque-looking lingerie, they went out together, shared quiet intimate dinners, or dinners that would have been quiet if it were not her doing the talking, opposite him, Zoned Out, looking at nothing, remembering nothing, feeling that each declarative sentence, each new conversational topic was some fresh Sisyphean effort, some heavy till she must put a strong shoulder into, to strike some pure note on the tuning fork, provoke some reaction in this vacant, this vapid, characterless man sitting across from her at some North or South Carolina bistro, a facsimile of some New York or LA bistro, themselves algorithmically optimized clones of some proto-colonized Michelin-rated locale, where indigenous food is made and served and consumed guiltlessly, without precision, by ordinary people, where everybody knows who he is and what is on the menu, where you do not have to ask. Quiet, content, it is not that he, Mark, seems dissatisfied or that she is afraid he's been unfaithful to her, if anything her feeling is that he lacks the critical imagination to even formulate a betrayal, that he doesn't possess sufficient force of character to even manage being unfaithful, that Julie in the middle of telling some story she has already forgotten the point of (having to do with a high school boyfriend, or a bad vacation or her car breaking down) studying her husband's tan face across the oil-stained tablecloth, cannot even formulate the question that needs answering.

The line cook will go first, doubtless imagining as he dissolves that whatever it is that swallows up his hands feet and throat, smooths his pores, seals his lips and melts his skin down, till he is just a pair of retinas trailing ocular nerves and pink-gray cerebrum floating there in front of now-burning shellfish, that whatever painlessly dissolves him is also part of some baleful conspiracy, some covert government action that has assumed him as its priority and target, as the real world never did, he is not alone in this. After all, when internal logics prove elusive, when mechanic and motive elide, you are left groping back for the rude sextant, the broadly-constituted State, the conspiratorial Oversoul, and certainly a number of observers, profiteers, hucksters and moon-eyed true believers will be clamorous to ascribe this secular meaning, to assert in earshot of the TV cameras and anyone else who'll listen, that this beige encroachment, this suffused and shapeless phenomenon, this big beige dissolve that captured five staff, ten diners, and several stray alley cats in its horrible throat, that it bears the distinct mark of some new biologic weapon, the attack of a foreign adversary, or experiment gone awry. Three minutes.

Bailey knocking his knee on the bottom of the table at once goes "Ow."

Julie petting her son's leg goes "What did I tell you."

The little boy with tears welling in his eyes says "Cunt cunt cunt cunt."

Several diners wheel around at the word. His mother gasps. His aunt's eyes widen, looking at her nephew, but then how can she possibly explain? Mark says "Bailey!" and then, almost as an after-thought "No!"

"Where did you learn that?" his mother asks her grip tightening, and Bailey, eyes widening, stares at his befuddled aunt. Something is going very wrong in the restaurant yes. The shellfish on the grill is burning. Water and chemicals leak from the storeroom. The kitchen is too quiet. Of course it is not the end of the world. It is just the end of this restaurant, this dinner, this evening which long should have ended. Then a flicker and the lights go out. And a few affrighted yips and laughs, where, before pulling out mobile phone lights, everyone is again a child. Then a great sense of movement, a muffled hurry and crash. And there is the waiter who'd misheard Julie's order, ogled her sister, splayed in a lump on the floor, groaning, trying to warn them all as people rush to his side, chatter to feel useful. Julie in the dark clutches her son close, looking at the waiter muttering through a broken nose on the ground in the dark. He is trying to tell them: *It is all dissolving around you* and: *It is so horrible* and *Good riddance to some of it*, he is trying to say, *A shame we can only remember the past and not the future*, but he doesn't manage any of it. What he says is: "Beige beige beige beige."

Herd

Yunya Yang

Yanzi became a resident at The Gift in March, when she had six months left, and now it is June.

"June!" a woman says to Yanzi at the weekly gathering. "How horrid. Do you know that my husband died in June? That's the only upside. Other than that, it's horrid."

Yanzi does know it, for she told her about him the first time they met, sitting under a palm tree by her mobile home. The Gift is full of mobile homes, most of them painted in pastel colors as if they were Easter eggs scattered on protected grass, waiting for some children to find them.

The woman's husband was a mechanic at an oil field. He fell into one of the tanks filled with a colorless, odorless, lethal chemical.

"There is a god," the woman declares. "He watches from seven feet above your head."

Others nod their agreement.

"We are the lucky ones," the leader of the gathering says. He is a priest of some sort, a devout man with unwavering beliefs. Yanzi thinks of him as inappropriately naive.

"I hear that elephants know when they're near the end. They walk away from their herd and go somewhere else to die," a young girl says. She is in a bright, traditional dress with sleeves that drape like a soft waterfall.

"Is a group of elephants called a herd?" someone asks.

"I think 'herd' is more for sheep…"

"Anything that doesn't know where it's going can be called a herd."

"But if the elephant knows…"

The discussion goes on for about half an hour until dinner is served. Yanzi goes to the gathering mainly for the food. She is tired of cooking and eating alone, but she is too hungry to skip meals altogether. In that sense, she still lives. Her will is either too strong or not strong enough.

The food served at the gathering is of a good variety. They get decent Chinese food sometimes, which is alarmingly close to the real thing. They get Peruvian or Thai or Ethiopian other times, which by the same logic should also be almost-authentic. That is all one can ask for at The Gift.

Yanzi is content. She doesn't really want something accurate or genuine, which can be insensitive and cruel. One time they ordered pho, and one of the residents fainted from just smelling the broth. Yanzi is glad it wasn't anything she has secretly hoped for. Who knows what would happen to her then? She doesn't want to embarrass herself in front of her new neighbors, who are her last companions.

At The Gift, it is always summer. The landscaping in the community is professionally done by a company called The Yard Brothers, and they come every Thursday to cut the grass and shape the bushes. Two deeply tanned men drive a white van from home to home, tending to the healthy and hopeful plants outside. The company's logo is stamped on the side of the van, a large, round design. A flower sits at the fork of the "Y" like a crown. Yanzi watches the van every week from her window. One of the men, one of the brothers, always waves at her. He later introduces himself as Jay and tells her that he was born and raised in the town.

"Have you ever thought about leaving?" she asks.

"I've got everything here, don't I?"

Yanzi is shocked and confused. She has never felt she's got everything anywhere.

When Yanzi was a little girl, she used to steal from a stationery store. It wasn't anything serious. She only took things that she thinks no one would miss. She stole a heart-shaped lock from a diary. She stole a small, spotted dog made of porcelain. She stole a toy pipe the size of her pinkie.

"But we are all guilty of certain desperation," she responds.

"Some trees can only survive in this climate," Jay says. "This is a good town for trees."

"Do you think you can plant a willow tree outside my home?" Yanzi asks.

"That's not local."

"You said it's good for trees here."

Jay frowns at Yanzi as if she had insulted him.

Yanzi goes back to her mobile home and resumes watching the brothers from the window. The white van reflects and redirects the harsh sunshine.

Yanzi thinks of earthworms drying on sidewalks after rain. The audacity of it, the despair.

It hasn't rained for many days.

At the end of July, Izaya moves into the baby blue mobile home next to Yanzi. He is a literary type. He wrote books and gave talks at universities. The books line the mahogany shelf in his living room, their spines beautifully hard and straight, climbed by fonts that command a certain authority.

"They *will* be my legacy," he says more to himself than to Yanzi.

"Of course," she obliges.

Izaya is confident that people would want to know his stories, that they are curious and kind. Yanzi indulges his fantasy. It is why she likes him, for we all need someone to remind us of the brighter side of things, whether or not there is indeed such a side.

She picks up cooking again. She used to cook for her husband, who often worked late. She would cover the dishes with a lime green food net to keep out flies. Sometimes she'd fall asleep waiting, but always woke at the crisp sound of a key turning in its matching lock. He's home, she'd think with breathless panic and glee.

Izaya tolerates Yanzi's cooking, but he'd rather eat elsewhere. He takes Yanzi to a fancy restaurant in town. Yanzi hasn't eaten anything outside of The Gift for months. Food outside is not for her, not in many ways. Of that, she is certain.

A long line outside of the restaurant loops around the corner, and some people have chairs and tents with them.

"It's very popular," Izaya says proudly.

Yanzi doesn't mind the wait. She's used to waiting. She's never in a hurry.

"You can eat the knives and forks," Izaya says. "They serve a dish that is pickled pigskin on a tree trunk. A tree trunk made of glass made of sugar made of mermaid tears."

"Mermaid tears are good for longevity," Yanzi says.

Izaya is not amused.

The priest who leads the gatherings at The Gift is not one of the residents, although he has always referred to himself as "we."

"We are the lucky ones."

"We are together."

"Shall we?"

It offers a sense of inclusiveness, which is of course false, but at least he has good intentions. He is warm and courteous to the residents. He is a good man, an upright man, who likely has their best interest at heart. However, Yanzi knows he would not hesitate to hurt or kill them under different circumstances.

The priest is eager to have Yanzi buy into his beliefs. "There is still a long way ahead of us," he says.

"In the heaving hills of Southern China, where the ground is covered by vigorous greenery, there is a clan of people who always bury their dead near home," Yanzi tells him.

The priest leans forward for the story. He thinks he is close to crack her.

"A shepherd of the dead would travel all over the country to bring back his deceased kinsmen. He would stand them up, tie them next to one another with ropes around their waists, and lead them back into the hills with a gentle tug."

"A shepherd," the priest says.

"Sometimes, the walk back takes years, decades."

The priest has tears in his eyes.

"But there is a distance one cannot walk."

The priest gasps.

Yanzi gets up for a second round of food. The priest trails behind her, looking for guidance.

Yanzi often keeps her windows open, but there is seldom any wind. The sun stands still in her brief home.

Outside, a commotion starts, and people are shouting with either excitement or horror, Yanzi can't tell which.

Is it time for the weekly gathering again? She has lost track of time passing. There is only day and night—the former improbably longer than the latter. She wakes in the morning, utterly oblivious.

But before the colorless light, in the folds of darkness, like so many others, she too dreams. She too sleeps safe and sound in her shell. She too longs to grow hoofs and horns and wings and leap forward a thousand miles through vast woodlands, along with her brothers and sisters, hurdling towards a destination where she is eagerly, eagerly expected.

the green of her

JILL KITCHEN

she of before is breathing still. a black swallowtail butterfly,
hers a gown you wish you could wear, striking gasps

into all who witness her shine, her silent song, this scalloped lace
edge of becoming. ancient blue dust brush, yellow wounds.

i remember. this body once cast from tree bark spoke the language
of branch, of root, of all the feathered earth whispered in the dark.

she drinks moonlight in her sleep above that red-split of heart-eye.
every secret the rain spilled in liquid tongues. a dream twinge of all

she once pulled close, cities she breathed into being. i am still that girl
of all things wild, of nettle & dock leaf, pitch pine & dogwood,

black raspberry thorns & wild garlic, fistfuls of grass from
the forest floor. what once she wore, what once she was. pirouette

of maple seeds forever falling. the way they silver they burn
they shudder to rise out of skin. how no one remembers the green

of her. the green of me. she breathes still. she breathes still.

Contributor Comments

Elena M. Aponte (she/her), "Vixen"

Elena M. Aponte is a writer and editor based in Michigan, and her work has appeared in The Indiana Review, *Barrelhouse,* Cartridge Lit, marrow magazine, *and elsewhere. She is a current MFA student in fiction at Vermont College of Fine Arts.*

Instagram: boricua_y_su_pajaro, Twitter: @PalanteAponte

I have always felt a kinship with foxes. They are misunderstood and dismissed as pests but have such a profound relationship with human folklore and mythology. I first saw them in the wild forests surrounding my bisabuelo's cabin Up North, on the outskirts of Traverse City, Michigan. I loved how freely they minded each other. Like how we all used to be as children, tumbling, nipping, sleeping in a cozy pile with our parents. I hope you see my appreciation for their playfulness and strength in this piece. We could stand to learn from their loyalty to each other.

William Archila, "Someone always came in"

William Archila is the author of The Art of Exile *and* The Gravedigger's Archaeology.

This quasi-sonnet is part of a series inspired by the pre-Columbian myth of El Cipitio, a Salvadorean figure generally portrayed as a naked boy with a big straw hat and deformed feet. He is the illegitimate son of a forbidden romance between an indigenous woman called Sihuehuet, now known as La Siguanaba, and her lover. As punishment for her infidelity, Teotl, the god of gods, condemned her to wander the ravines and rivers at night, while the boy was sentenced to eternal youth. Today La Siguanaba is a shape-changing spirit washing clothes by the riverside and enchanting men lost in the countryside.

Photo credit: Lory Bedikian

Mark Bessen (he/him), "The False Prophet of New Beginnings"

Mark Bessen is a queer writer based in Austin, Texas.

This story grew out of my interest in exploring how mental illness can shape the way we construct (and destruct) the realities around us. I was drawn to the challenge of rendering the voice of a character in an altered mental state within the confines of a realistic story in which that character is our only conduit of information. I wrote "The False Prophet of New Beginnings" to embody the hope, excitement, and desperation of a character simultaneously experiencing mania and striving for a fresh start.

Jennifer Blackman (She/her), "She Could Do What She Wanted"

Jennifer Blackman's flash has appeared with American Short Fiction, Tin House, *and* McSweeney's, *her longer stories in* Epiphany Magazine *and* Nimrod, *among others. A copy editor at* The New Yorker, *she lives in Austin with her husband and their bloodthirsty cat.*

I was at the tail end of a weeklong stay with friends in New Hampshire, in September of 2020, when a neighborly picnic fell into place. A simple thing, made electric with autumn rushing in, cider-pressing, all that glorious picture-book folksy stuff, and a pandemic. Writing in my apartment the next morning, back in a city of locked doors and forbidding stairwells, I wanted to continue having my fun, to be among friends and in love with my friends. I wanted that charge. And my mind began circling around risk–the picnic had been my first in six months—and how we calculate risk, and how easy it might be to miss one risk while looking out for another.

Amber Blaeser-Wardzala (she/her), "What They Don't Teach You in Catholic School"

Amber Blaeser-Wardzala, an MFA Fiction Candidate at Arizona State University, is an Anishinaabe writer, beader, fencer, and Jingle Dress Dancer from White Earth Nation in Minnesota.
Website: amberblaeserwardzala.wordpress.com, Instagram and Twitter: @amber2dawn

I went to a conservative, almost all-white, Catholic school for thirteen years. As you would imagine, there wasn't proper sex-ed, but more than that, there was little education on the functions of a female body. Between the Catholic propaganda about sex, my school's gatekeeping of how my body works, and the trauma of being bullied for being biracial, I came out of high school with a warped relationship to sex, my body, and myself that I continue to work to undo.

Photo credit: Kimberly M. Blaeser

Allison Blevins (she/her) and Joshua Davis (he/him), "Letters from One Disabled Body to Another Disabled Body"

Allison Blevins is a queer disabled writer and the author of Cataloguing Pain *(YesYes Books, 2023),* Handbook for the Newly Disabled, A Lyric Memoir *(BlazeVox, 2022), and* Slowly/Suddenly *(Vegetarian Alcoholic Press, 2021).*
allisonblevins.com
Joshua Davis is the author of Reversal Spells in Blue and Black *(Seven Kitchens Press, 2022) and* Chorus for the Kill *(Seven Kitchens Press, 2022), and he offers online workshops at The Poetry Barn and teaches high school English near Tampa, Florida.*
Website: joshuadavispoet.com

This piece developed as part of our chapbook *fiery poppies bruising their own throats* (Glass Lyre Press, forthcoming). Like all literary voices, the voices in the letters are masks, are made, crafted, but as we wrote, we began to understand we were revealing more than normal, and when the exposure turned scary, we focused on each other's letters. We asked, "What should I not say?"

And then we said it. The aim was to write replies our letters deserved and needed. We've known each other so long the letters poured out as a literary extension of our daily conversation.

Demetrius Buckley, (he/him), "Porous Rock"

Demetrius Buckley is the winner of the 2021 Toi Derricotte &Cornelius Eady Chapbook Prize, and his work has appeared or is forthcoming in the Michigan Quarterly Review, *where he won the 2020 Page Davidson Clayton Prize for Emerging Poets,* Apogee, PEN America, *and* RHINO. *Website: demetriusbuckley.com*

"Porous Rock" is an approximation of the urban plight. The characters described in the poem claim their own origins. Like grandmas, women of religious stern, hands were always oily. But the men, the failed warriors in this poem, reconstruct trauma as a norm, "a prison release form framed," followed by career options. In the end, the incarcerated becomes a kind of porous rock, alive but motionless in the time given, and the letter in the end was written by a prisoner to himself and to the men in the poem, an ode to our ancient Diaspora.

Image credit: Daniella Toosie-Watson (this is a recent portrait instead of a photograph because of the limits of Demetrius' incarceration)

Ayn Carrillo-Gailey (she/her), "Prologue to 'The Wildings,' a novel in progress"

Ayn was the recipient of the Tahoma Literary Review *Fellowship to the Mineral School arts residency. Her non-fiction work has been published in* Elle (UK), Latina, *and* Kinfolk *and her memoir,* Pornology, *was adapted to film in 2020.*
Website: ayngailey.com, Instagram: @ayngailey.
Learn more about the annual Tahoma Literary Review *Fellowship at mineral-school.org/residency/residency-fellowships*

This story was inspired by my belief that food is so much more than a base need. It is also language, culture, and a way to express love. My character hunts for lost recipes and foods going extinct while she grapples with the loss of her most significant relationship and the disappearance of her Chinese mother, who is depressed in a culture that doesn't have a word for that.

Michael Czyzniejewski, (he/him), "Over and Over, But Only Much, Much Later"

Michael Czyzniejewski's fourth collection of stories, The Amnesiac in the Maze, *will appear in 2023 from Braddock Avenue Books.*
Twitter: @MCzyzniejewski

There was a time when I played a lot of ball and shot a hundred free throws a day. My record was 78/100. A friend of mine who played ball in high school went with me to shoot around and he shot 96—he hadn't played in years. This was the end of my free throw obsession.

Photo credit: Karen Craigo

Julia Kolchinsky Dasbach, (she/her), "Why write another poem about the moon?"

Julia Kolchinsky Dasbach emigrated from Ukraine at age six and is the author of three poetry collections, most recently 40 WEEKS *(YesYes Books, 2023).*
Website: juliakolchinskydasbach.com, Facebook: @jkolch, Instagram and Twitter: @jkdpoetry

The series of poems all with the shared title "Why write another poem about the moon?" come from my next full-length book manuscript. It grapples with the experience of raising a neurodiverse child on the autism spectrum with a disabled partner. The way poets are obsessed with turning to the moon, so too, I cannot stop writing about motherhood. The poems embrace the parallels between motherhood and moon—the way both rise, set, wax, and wane. The way mother, like moon, is always there—worrying, spinning, pulling tides—mothering, even when we cannot see her.

Photo credit: Connor North Goad

Sean Thomas Dougherty, (he/him), "Arrangement and Lament with Voiceless Bilabial Plosives"

Sean Thomas Dougherty is the author or editor of 19 books including The Dead are Everywhere Telling Us Things *(2021 Jacar Press).*
Website: seanthomasdoughertypoet.com

The poem started just as it does, when the first couplet arrived with the rain. I was on break at work on third shift and it was raining hard outside. I wrote down fast the first couplet on the back of a med form. I added the linguistic name for "p" sounds later for the title.

Photo Credits: Melanie Rae Buonavolonta

Naihobe González, "To the Man on the Greyhound to Montréal"

Naihobe González is a Venezuelan-American writer currently based in Mexico City, at work on her first novel.
Twitter: @nai__gonzalez

This essay was inspired by the Letter to a Stranger column published by *Off Assignment*, the travel writing magazine. The column (which has been anthologized) is based on a simple but powerful question: "Who haunts you?" When I thought back to my travels, the man on the Greyhound bus to Montréal immediately surfaced. This essay was a way to explore why he had haunted me so, and through him, reflect on the complexities of moving through the world as a young woman, alone.

Julia Halprin Jackson, (she/her), "A Posse of Parables"

Julia Halprin Jackson is the co-founder and publicity director of Play On Words, San Jose's collaborative literary performance series, and a 2021-2023 Lighthouse Book Projecteer. Website: juliahalprinjackson.com, Twitter: @Juliahj

As a graduate student at UC Davis, one of my professors challenged me to compress my work into as small a form as I could imagine. I became obsessed with writing 100-word stories—and eventually wrote 100 of them. I love the economy and impact that each word has when limited to such short forms.

Photo credit: Mimi Carroll

Lisa Beech Hartz, (she/her), "Her Rain Is My Rain"

Lisa Beech Hartz directs Seven Cities Writers project which brings cost-free workshops to underserved communities. Website: 7cwp.org, Facebook: sevencitieswriters

My mother, like too many elderly people, lives with dementia which has robbed her of her memory and slowly over time, of herself. It is a terrifying and perversely fascinating thing to witness. Where did all that long life go? What can be salvaged from it? This poem is part of a working manuscript, "Old Love," which explores life-long love relationships—marriage, parenthood—and what keeps us bound together across a lifetime. What is love without memory? Without story?

Kalila Holt, (she/her), "How to Die"

Kalila Holt has been previously published in wigleaf, Salamander, *and* The Los Angeles Review, *among others, and also produces the podcast "Heavyweight."*
Twitter: @kalilaholt

When I was in high school, I started writing a piece about suicide that I quickly abandoned—it just made me too uncomfortable. Since then, I've had several very close relationships with people struggling with depression. It's a dynamic I've had a hard time grappling with, and one I wanted to try writing about, so I salvaged a small part of that high school piece for this story.

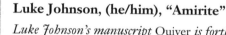

Luke Johnson, (he/him), "Amirite"

Luke Johnson's manuscript Quiver *is forthcoming fall 2023 from Texas Review Press.*
You can find more of his work at his website.
Website: lukethepoet.com, Twitter: @Lukesrant, Instagram: lukejohnsonpoetry

"Amirite" was born out of a lyric impulse. Most often my poems arrive and it's up to me to make myself available to them. What I found early on, was that Amirite's impulse was informed by a growing frustration around the intersection of American patriotism and nationalism. How boys' bodies are historically used as a currency of war and how all of us: fathers, mothers, etc., etc. are equally implicated in that reality. "Amirite" let's nobody off. It's an anti-love, love poem of sorts. A reluctant mistress.

Jill Kitchen, (she/her), "the green of her"

Jill Kitchen lives in Boulder, Colorado where she can be found rollerskating on the creek path searching for great horned owls; her work appears or is forthcoming in Ecotone, Parentheses, The Penn Review, Pidgeonholes, Radar Poetry, Rust + Moth, The Shore, SWWIM, Whale Road Review *and elsewhere. Website: linktr.ee/jillkitchen, Facebook: jillkitchen, Instagram: @msjillkitchen, Twitter: @jillkitchen*

This poem came to light after seeing a photograph a neighbor shared of a black swallowtail butterfly she had seen in her garden. I was obsessed with the detail of the wings. I thought of how the butterfly carries her caterpillar days within her, unseen, unremembered by others. The rest of the poem came more than six months later, when I connected it to my own childhood, to the young and wild within me. It feels like the part of us that often feels the most ourselves comes from those early years, from that "green" time.

Konstantin Kulakov (he/they), "Neon Hymn: Excerpt"

Konstantin Kulakov (he/they) is a poet and translator born in Zaoksky, Soviet Union. His poems and translations appear or are forthcoming in Witness, Jet Fuel Review, Spillway, Phoebe, Harvard Journal of African American Policy, Passengers Journal, *and* Loch Raven Review, *among others. They hold an MFA in Creative Writing from Naropa University and are co-founding editor of* Pocket Samovar *magazine. They live in Washington, D.C., on occupied Piscataway and Anacostan land.*
Website: konstantinkulakov.com, Instagram: @kmkulakov

These poems are from my manuscript "Neon Hymn" and seek to reckon with the pressures of post-Soviet migration and intergenerational memory. They share a similar aspiration: a lyric interrogation of whiteness and ask, "What is left of the post-Soviet identity after acculturation and how can this identity sustain an ethical counterforce to racial capitalism?" Bilingual grammars, a familial lineage of dissent, and prayer as counterpart to resistance proved essential to finding my footing. The poems also owe much to Jeffrey Pethybridge, Claudia Rankine, James H. Cone, and of course, my grandfather and gulag survivor Mikhail P. Kulakov, who all—directly or indirectly—shaped their coming to be.

Photo credit: Jared Siskin

Nathan Manley, "Woodhouse's Toad, *Anaxyrus woodhousii*"

Nathan Manley is a writer, translator, erstwhile English teacher, and freshly minted attorney whose poems and Latin translations appear in a wide variety of journals, both online and in print.
Website: nathanmmanley.com

"Woodhouse's Toad" is one poem from a sequence in which I'm exploring the ecology of the Great Plains. These particular organisms thrive abundantly in northern Colorado, where I lived for many years and often startled one as it hunkered beneath a spigot in my garden. The inciting thought, as I began to consider any possible connection between the life of a toad and my own, was that the toad's experience must be strange to mine in like quality and proportion as the toad's to a stone's—that is to say, irretrievably strange. The poem seems to discover that my recognition of our mutual alienation, that sense of one's utter smallness in a cosmic scheme of things, could never really amount to love.

David McDannald, "Written as Malaria Hit"

After close to six years on the Navajo Nation in Arizona, David McDannald recently relocated with his wife and daughter to Western Mass.
Website: davidmcdannald.com, Twitter: @dkmcdannald

My attempts to befriend the Baka and Bayaka several times got me threatened by the Bantu, the dominant tribe. "It's not safe for you to stay here," a man warned me in a remote town in Gabon. The conflict was one-sided but as old as that between farmers and hunters. When I heard there were Baka living alone at Ngato Ancien, I hired a motorcycle to make the long trip through the jungle. Back in Yaoundé, at the capital's lone coffee shop, I wrote the first lines of this essay and realized I had a fever. I spent the next two days in bed, fortunate to be able to afford malaria's ten dollar cure.

Photo Credits: Richard Sparkman

Caite McNeil, (she/her), "Killing Time"

Caite McNeil is an author and illustrator who lives in Midcoast Maine with her husband and young child. Website: caitemcneil.com

In writing and drawing my stories, I keep coming back to interrogate the state of motherhood and a mother's identity. Throughout that exploration, anxiety swirls: about mortality (my own, my parents', my child's), about the climate crisis and the doomed planet of our children's future, about the performative nature of motherhood today, and my hunch that I'll never be good enough. I think my work also attempts to elevate and find beauty in the mundanity of parenthood. This piece asks: is it possible to find spiritual transcendence while on a walk through a graveyard with a toddler and a dog?

Dion O'Reilly, (she/they), "Right to Life"

Dion O'Reilly, the author of Ghost Dogs, *a teacher and podcaster, splits her time between a farm in Santa Cruz, CA, and a tiny home in Bellingham, WA.*
Website: dionoreilly.wordpress.com, Facebook: @dionlissner-oreilly, Instagram: @deepobrain, Twitter: @dionoreilly

This poem—written right after the Dobbs decision—began as a contemplation of the war against women's bodies, and how, for me, hatred of my body originated with my mother. Here is the beginning of the first draft which might become its own poem someday: I step into the day, peel the night from my fat belly and loose thighs, an old woman now I don't know how to look upon myself (please) with any kind of love. Oh mother, I see you in the right to life, the many fingers pointing at the wombs of women...

Photo credit: Michael Cox

Shannon Huffman Polson, (she/her), "There Is Smoke in Brooklyn"

Shannon Huffman Polson is a writer of nonfiction and poetry focusing on the natural world, faith, women and war; her books include North of Hope: A Daughter's Arctic Journey *and* The Grit Factor: Courage, Resilience and Leadership in the Most Male Dominated Organization in the World. *Website: shannonpolson.com, Twitter: @aborderlife, Instagram: @aborderlife, @shannonhpolson*

"There Is Smoke in Brooklyn" responds to the author and her family's direct experience of wildfire in North Central Washington, while compelled equally by their connection to global climate change and the complicated interface of humans and the wild.

Jesse Salvo, (he/him), "Beige, Beige, Beige, Beige"

Jesse Salvo is a native New Yorker but now lives in Seville, Spain. His work has been published in over a dozen literary journals including Hobart Pulp, Maudlin House, Barren Magazine, Menacing Hedge, X-Ray Lit, *others. His first novel,* Blue Rhinoceros, *debuted in May 2022 courtesy of New Meridian Arts. Salvo serves as senior fiction editor and contributing columnist for* Bull Magazine. *Website: jessesalvowrites.com, Instagram: blue_rhinoceros_book*

I was on a turbulent flight from Texas to NY in between book events and the pilot came on to announce that there was a backup on the tarmac at our destination, we were running out of fuel and would need to divert course and land at a nearby airport. Suddenly the idea came to me of this small family unit, with all the banal troubles that plague small families, sitting in a restaurant and being told that their surroundings are about to dissolve. It seemed, of course, absurd and a little morbid, but also sort of grimly compelling. The plane eventually landed safely. By the time it did, I had jotted down the first draft of this story.

April Meredith Thompson, (she/her), "Obsession"

April Meredith Thompson is a writer, who lives and works on the unceded Musqueam, Squamish, and Tsleil-Waututh territory in Vancouver, Canada.

In this piece I was interested in the archaeology of a very eighties perfume—and the way fragrance advertising obsesses over female sexuality. The use of perfume to hunt a wild tiger was a unique backdrop to explore the line between extinction and revival, predator and prey.

Photo credit: Brittany Lucas

Sherre Vernon, (she/her), "Open, Persephone Ate It"

Sherre Vernon (she/her), the award-winning author of Green Ink Wings *(Elixir Press) and* The Name is Perilous *(Power of Poetry), explores motherhood, identity and generational healing in her first full-length collection of poetry,* Flame Nebula, Bright Nova *(Main Street Rag).*
Website: sherrevernon.com, all social media platforms: @sherrevernon

When my daughter was four, she cried herself awake, fearing her death and my own. It shook me. That same week, I saw her pulling pomegranates from the bush in our yard and eating them. I was flooded with Demeter's grief at the loss of her daughter to the underworld. Here it was again: the fruit, a mother's heartbreak, and then the wrenching parallel to Eve being cast out. How brave we must be to stumble through life as women. So much sacrifice. Perhaps the only way we survive our losses is believing our daughters will return to spring.

Photo Credits: Sherre Vernon

Lisbeth White, (she/her), "Migratory Animals"

Lisbeth White, author of American Sycamore *(Perugia Press 2022), is a writer and ritualist living on S'Klallam and Chimacum lands of the Olympic Peninsula.*
Website: lisbethwrites.com, IG: @earthmaven

I've always found the moments of coming across wild animals killed by cars particularly painful. The suddenness of the violence, both the reckless nature of our human movements and the quickness of the passing, is so jarring yet becomes commonplace. The brevity of this piece is an attempt to capture the reverberations we experience—in our bodies, in our senses of safety, in our cultures—as we witness continual and continuous bursts of violence and its aftermath.

Photo credit: Sarah Wright Photography

Yunya Yang, (she/her), "Herd"

Yunya Yang's work appears in Split Lip Magazine, Gulf Coast, The Baltimore Review, *among others.*
Twitter @YangYunya

Joy Williams is one of the inspirations of the story. Another is old Chinese folklore. As an immigrant, I always find myself exploring the theme of being an outsider, an alien. Even after years of living in a different country, even after the changes in habits, friends, and beliefs, some things stick around. There is always home, and it is always elsewhere.

CPSIA information can be obtained
at www.ICGtesting.com
Printed in the USA
LVHW081124150323
741648LV00009B/561

9 781736 575086